UNHOLY LIES

UNHOLY LIES

SANDRA BRETTING

FIVE STAR

A part of Gale, Cengage Learning

GALE
CENGAGE Learning®

Detroit • New York • San Francisco • New Haven, Conn • Waterville, Maine • London

GALE
CENGAGE Learning

LIBRARY OF CONGRESS CATALOGING-IN-PUBLICATION DATA

Bretting, Sandra.
    Unholy lies / Sandra Bretting. — 1st ed.
      p. cm.
    ISBN 978-1-4328-2597-3 (hardcover) — ISBN 1-4328-2597-6 (hardcover)
      1. Women journalists—Texas—Fiction. I. Title.
    PS3602.R4586U54 2012
    813'.6—dc23   2012017263

First Edition. First Printing: October 2012.
Published in conjunction with Tekno Books and Ed Gorman.
Find us on Facebook– https://www.facebook.com/FiveStarCengage
Visit our website– http://www.gale.cengage.com/fivestar/
Contact Five Star™ Publishing at FiveStar@cengage.com

Printed in Mexico
1 2 3 4 5 6 7 16 15 14 13 12

For Roger, a True Gentleman

ACKNOWLEDGMENTS

Like any interesting journey, writing a book involves sometimes stopping to ask for directions along the way. I have been blessed to meet amazing navigators on my journey who have selflessly pointed me in the right direction.

First and foremost is my decades-long writing partner, Susan Breeden. Thank you, Susan, for sharing your wisdom and your talent, both of which are boundless. Your incredible way with words is matched only by the beauty of your gentle spirit.

Thank you also to members of the Heart of Texas Chapter of Sisters in Crime for accepting *Unholy Lies* into the Barbara Burnett Smith Aspiring Writers Project. Under the watchful eye of the late Micqui Miller, the manuscript found its path. I also am indebted to member and author Russ Hall for his willingness to work with newcomers on the road as such a wonderful editor and coach.

For providing an aerial view of the whole process, thanks goes out to members of the Writers' League of Texas. The League's conferences and workshops—not to mention the camaraderie of other writers—has been invaluable.

Thank you to my editor, Alice Duncan, for shining up the manuscript once the journey was complete. To friends and colleagues whom I haven't named, please know that I've treasured your input. And always, to my daughters, Brooke and Dana . . . thank you for being the best inspiration of all. I love you more than you will ever know.

PROLOGUE

LilliFay Holiday entered the church, savoring every step. She had come once before like this, on a Friday, when the place stood utterly still. Oh, the organist might come later to practice some hymns, or a Sunday School teacher could show up to plot out the next grade-school pageant. To be truthful, that was always a painful experience, what with the children's whisper-thin voices torturing even the simplest of songs.

When she closed her eyes, LilliFay could hear echoes of her husband Bobby's sermons reverberating from the walls. She had memorized her favorite one; she knew every line by heart. She had stood at the podium during her last visit and repeated each sentence, letter perfect, to an imaginary audience. It made her feel so close to God and even a little closer to her husband. Wasn't that almost the same thing?

She tiptoed down the center aisle to where the pulpit stood. She felt a little guilty, sneaking around like this on a weekday, when Bobby was probably cloistered in his office, agonizing over his sermon. But it was her church, too. Why, what with Bobby traveling and all, preaching in other towns, maybe it was more her church than his because she never missed a Sunday, no matter how obscure the pastor who would be called in to preach for Bobby.

She bowed her head solemnly. She would pray for Bobby's soul. Again. Beseech God to make him see the error of his ways. Make him see that nothing good could have come from this nonsense of his with Becca Cooper, the young woman who played piano for them every Sunday morning. Since Becca showed up in Enterprise, things had been different between her and Bobby. Why couldn't they go back to the way things were? She tucked her head lower, determined to pray all the harder.

"LilliFay?"

She glanced toward the sound. "George Hines! Shame on you for scaring me like that." Her eyes narrowed. "If you can't tell, I'm trying to pray."

The police sergeant knelt beside her.

"Shouldn't you be out doing your job?" She'd done nothing wrong coming into the church. It was her right as a preacher's wife.

"I came to find you, LilliFay."

"How'd you know I was here?" Of all the places for someone to look, she didn't think this would be the very first.

"I checked the house, but you weren't there."

"It doesn't matter, you've found me. Now you can go away."

George squinted up at the stained glass. "It's not that simple. I've come to talk to you." He rubbed his hands together. "We got a call from headquarters. The Coopers filed a missing person's report on their daughter, Becca. You'll have to come with me."

CHAPTER 1

The tap of her finger against the computer keyboard felt solid. Kelsey Garrett pounded out the last sentence in her newspaper story, then shoved the chair back from her desk. *What a rush.*

The first time she felt the adrenaline flow, it was like soaring, like she could write a hundred stories and see her byline appear a hundred times. That was five years ago, when she was a lowly college freshman at the University of Houston. That feeling kept her working as a reporter, though, first at a throwaway in the Valley, then here at the *Enterprise Country Caller Gazette.* Grinding away for $20,000 a year, when even her college advisor had run for the safety of public relations and its fat paychecks. He'd call her sometimes—using a $200 cell phone, no doubt—and brag about taking a client to lunch at the Twelve Oaks Grill or Pierre's in Houston, when she barely had enough pocket change for the Grande Burrito next door.

Her jealousy faded only when she scooped up the latest issue of the *Enterprise Country Caller* from the door mat. Tuesday and Saturday mornings, come rain or shine. She liked to cut out her articles over breakfast and slip them into a phony leather portfolio she kept stashed under her bed. That book, her portfolio, was her ticket out of Enterprise, Texas, to exotic destinations like the *Houston Sentinel,* the *Dallas Daily Post,* or maybe, someday, the *Los Angeles Review.*

Now, sitting at her desk and scanning the first line of the story, she squirmed. The Enterprise police department never did call her back, and the details were pretty sketchy at this point. But deadlines were deadlines, and the newsroom's clock didn't care about unsubstantiated sources; it only clicked closer and closer to the end of the day. This story, her story, had all the trappings of a front-page feature. The only reason she'd even named a suspect in the woman's disappearance was because of the suspect's husband, Reverend Robert Holiday. Even her editor would come around when she saw such a famous pastor's wife was involved in the crime.

Nope, she had nothing to feel guilty about. It was probably only adrenaline causing her foot to tap-dance against the floor. She scanned the computer screen for typos for the fifth time. This story definitely deserved a slot in her portfolio.

Local Woman Missing

May 11—Enterprise law enforcement agents confirmed today the disappearance of local resident Becca Cooper, 28. Cooper, musical accompanist at Second Coming Charismatic Church, was last seen four days ago following Sunday services.

A native of Broken Arrow, Oklahoma, Cooper relocated to Enterprise last year. Police say the woman's family reported her missing when daily telephone calls went unanswered.

While police have not yet released information regarding suspects in the case, local sources confirm LilliFay Holiday, spouse of senior pastor Robert Holiday, has been questioned as a person of interest.

"There's not much to tell right now," said Sergeant George Hines. "All I can say is we haven't ruled out foul play."

Police plan to make a public appeal for information on Cooper's disappearance within the next few days, Hines said.

Nope, she had nothing to feel guilty about. With one tap of the "send" key, the story shot into her editor's terminal over ethereal fiber optic strands. She could go home now, back to the hundred-year-old cottage she rented just a few blocks away from the newspaper building.

She leaned back and laced her fingers behind her neck. She might even head over to the Grande Burrito next door for the Friday special first, maybe talk to the owner, Bernie, a bit. Now that her work was done, it was time for a cold beer.

LilliFay watched soap bubbles swirl in her kitchen sink, her fingertips shriveled from washing them. Still, she felt dirty.

Sergeant Hines had insisted she come back with him to the police station. He even drove her over there in his squad car, which was sitting right out in front of the sanctuary, for all the world to see. The car's bright decals and amber lights looked profane compared to the beige bricks of the building. It had stopped LilliFay cold; it was like seeing a hearse drive down the highway in the bright May sun.

The squad car was clean enough on the outside, but it was a mess on the inside, with flesh-colored upholstery worn thin in spots, an ashtray belching cigarette butts smoked down to the nub, and a fat notebook wedged between the two front seats, next to a rumpled bag of potato chips and a pockmarked foam coffee cup. All this was under a tangle of black plastic cords that webbed the inside roof. The car was so disorganized, Sergeant Hines probably told anyone who would listen that it wasn't his fault he couldn't find a blessed thing in there.

She'd slid into the car's backseat and hugged the side door all the way to the police station. She could only imagine what common criminals had touched the very same vinyl. Sergeant Hines asked her if she wanted her husband, Bobby, to come along, but that would only make things worse, so she said no, she'd handle this on her own.

Besides, once again, Bobby would come across as caring, worried. While, once again, she'd be the one with the problem.

Just like when the Spirit moved her to drop to her knees in church and people would start snickering in the pews behind her. Or, when the migraines came over her on Wednesday nights and she just couldn't make it to the women's Bible study. They finally stopped calling her by the end of the Old Testament. Even the church's choir director wouldn't talk to her anymore. Was it her fault she and Bobby had failed to produce an heir to round out the chorus of chubby angels singing glory to God in the highest for the Christmas pageant? No, *she* was always the one with the problem. *Poor Bobby,* she could only imagine the parishioners whisper behind her back.

So she went by herself to the police station, and she came home by herself. Now, as she watched bubbles spiral down the sink's drain, her energy seemed to flow with them. Her shoulders sagged when the front door creaked open.

"LilliFay?"

She turned, and there was Bobby, frowning, his eyebrows drawn together. It took the breath right out of her.

"Did you forget something?" She tried to fold her arms, but the skin on her hands was raw, so she let them hang loose at her sides.

"I didn't forget anything. I came home early so I could talk to you."

"So, talk."

He held out his hand, but she ignored it. She walked to the breakfast table and slid out one of the pine chairs. Was it time for dinner yet? She wasn't the slightest bit hungry.

"Sergeant Hines called me. What's going on?"

Now it was her turn. "Apparently Enterprise's finest thinks I know where Becca Cooper is. As if I'm in charge of that woman's schedule." LilliFay didn't sit down; she couldn't bear it if Bobby sat next to her.

"Well, do you?"

She steadied her hand on the back of the chair. She should walk away now; she should let the words remain unsaid. To speak up would change everything. "Of course not, Bobby. I could ask the same question of you." He stared at her as if she were speaking in tongues. "I know about you and Becca. I've always known. Your secretary told me a long time ago." There. Now that she had said it, there was no going back.

"Oh, my." Bobby shut his eyes.

"Did you really think you could keep it a secret?" She pressed harder and harder against the back of the chair, even though doing so hurt her fingers. She could snap that chair in two. "Who do you think made sure no one else reserved the church's condo on Thursday nights so you'd have some privacy? All this time, your secretary's been covering for you. Not that you deserved it."

Slowly, he opened his eyes. "LilliFay, sweetheart—"

"Don't, Bobby. Worst part is, even the deacons knew. Harris told me months ago I should up and leave you. Said I deserved better. Guess everyone knew." She tucked a strand of gray-brown hair behind her ear. What did it matter now? "Only no one would say anything to you."

"I can explain—"

"Really? You can explain this? Please, by all means." Only then did she pull out the chair and sit down.

"I didn't want to spend time with Becca. I felt sorry for her. You know, what with her getting divorced and all."

LilliFay laughed. "Didn't she get divorced a while ago, back in Oklahoma? It's an awful long time to be so broken up about it." Bobby's lips were parted slightly and she heard his breath, quick and shallow. "All you had to do was tell me. Was that so hard? Just tell me."

"I should get back to the church," he mumbled. "Deacons' meeting is tonight. They'll probably have a lot of questions."

15

No, you should be with me, she wanted to scream. But she didn't. "If that's what you think is best."

Bobby turned to leave. Hard as she tried, much as she wanted to, she felt the pull of him, and she couldn't quite stop the words, which tumbled from her lips. "Bobby, let me at least fix you a sandwich."

CHAPTER 2

Kelsey peered through the passenger window of her car at an address on the putty-colored brick wall. The minute she heard the news on the police scanner, just as she was leaving the newsroom for the day, she knew the Grande Burrito would have to wait.

Luckily, everyone seemed to know where to find Reverend Holiday's house: two left turns, then one to the right. Look for the house with the large wooden cross on the front door, she'd been told.

The house she found by taking two left turns and one right had neatly manicured, though browning, grass and a carefully tended flower border. A pin oak cast long shadows over its roof and the frilled edge of a baby-blue curtain peeked through a window. Nothing stirred in the stifling heat.

She stepped from the car and walked toward the ranch house. When she knocked, a deadbolt clicked open, exposing about a quarter of an older woman's face. A braided metal chain kept the lady from opening the door further.

"Mrs. Holiday? May I speak with you a moment?"

The door slammed shut, and she worried that maybe she'd be left to swelter in the early evening sun. But after a moment, she heard the rustle of a metal chain and the door swung open. LilliFay Holiday stood in the entrance, wearing a flower print housedress and rectangular eyeglasses with sequined butterflies glued to each corner.

"Are you a member of the congregation?" She appraised Kelsey from behind the cat's-eye glasses.

"Why, yes. Yes, I am," Kelsey lied. Anything to get away from the blistering sun and into the coolness of the foyer.

The woman opened the door and Kelsey stepped over the threshold. A wooden hat rack crisscrossed behind an old bureau that held a Bible and a rotary phone. The place smelled of dust. She followed as LilliFay walked stiffly through the foyer and into a shadowed living room. Dozens of plaster figurines— cherubs, mostly—had been nailed to the room's walls, and behind the figures, thin veins of gold foil dribbled down shimmery aqua wallpaper. A cobalt carpet, wall-to-wall, completed the theme of blue. It looked like nothing new had been added to the room in a good forty years.

LilliFay wiped her hands on an apron she wore over her housedress. She seemed to have remembered she was a pastor's wife, after all, because she smiled at Kelsey, and pointed to a portrait in a simple tin frame. It was a picture of LilliFay standing behind a man, her teased hair upswept, her mouth unsmiling as she gazed into the camera. In contrast, her companion wore a broad smile; his eyes sparkled like a friendly grandfather's.

"I'm sure you know my husband, then," LilliFay said, gesturing toward the picture. "Let's go into the living room, shall we?"

Kelsey gazed at the picture as she made her way to the living room. She couldn't help but notice that in the portrait, LilliFay's hand hovered over her husband's left shoulder, her fingertips not quite grazing his suit jacket. As if she was uncomfortable about touching her own husband.

"Bobby's got that new cable television show, so he stays pretty busy. Now, what can I do for you?" She pointed to a blue velvet recliner, and Kelsey sat down.

"I came to talk to you about Becca Cooper."

"Oh." Her smile slipped sideways. "Whatever for?" She sank into a worn couch opposite Kelsey, and covered her knees with her housedress.

"I just heard something on the police scanner. They found a woman's body earlier, in the bayou. Young woman, late twenties. Sounds a lot like that missing person—Becca Cooper."

LilliFay gasped. "No." Her fingers fluttered to her lips. "That can't be!"

"Somehow, they think you had something to do with her disappearance, Mrs. Holiday. Now, why would they think that?"

Instead of answering her, LilliFay focused on the flock of cherubs hanging on the wall behind Kelsey's head. She seemed to gather strength from the plaster figures. Finally, she found her voice.

"Who did you say you were again? I don't think I like this line of questioning. Are you sure you're from the church?"

This time Kelsey didn't have the heart to lie. "No, ma'am. I'm a reporter, for the *Country Caller Gazette*."

"Well, you're not a very good one, are you?"

Kelsey blinked. She'd expected to be kicked out of the house, or at least berated right then and there. What she didn't expect was to be called out for her journalism skills. "Excuse me?"

"You don't ask the suspect about a crime. Didn't they teach you that in journalism school?" LilliFay rolled her eyes. "Honestly, what are they teaching folks in those liberal colleges?"

"Mrs. Holiday, this is serious. I thought you might want to set the record straight for our readers."

LilliFay waved aside the comment. "Not on your life. Now . . . there's a right way and a wrong way to go about this. If you're going to do it right, at least put your back into it. Don't you have a notebook? You might want to write this down."

Kelsey gulped, unaccustomed to taking orders from an interview subject. LilliFay didn't seem all that concerned the police might have found Becca Cooper's body.

"First, you have to find all the suspects. All of them." She rose to her feet. "Now, nothing like this has happened in Enterprise in a looonnnggg time, but that doesn't mean there aren't a dozen people who wouldn't like to do the very same thing. If only they thought they could get away with it." She began to pace the river of carpet, her brow furrowed. "You'll want to check out all the angles. Even the ones you don't think look promising. Just because we're a ways from Houston doesn't mean we don't have our share of drama."

Kelsey reached for a reporter's notebook she kept in the front pocket of her purse and a pen she'd stashed in her khakis, just in case. She never knew when someone might say something interesting, and it paid to be prepared.

"Now, Becca was new in town, no doubt about that," LilliFay continued. "Most families have lived around here since before their granddaddies. And, pretty. No denying that, either." She paused, acutely aware of her words now. "It doesn't help she was a single gal among all of us married folk. No, that doesn't help her case one bit." The bluster began to ebb from her voice. "Let me tell you this, though. Some people do things so terrible it's only right to want to hurt them back. Even the Bible says an eye for an eye."

At that moment, LilliFay withdrew a thin black Bible from the pocket of her apron. She began to flip through the worn pages, and stopped about one-fourth of the way through. "Here it is. Moses on Mt. Sinai. What did you say your name was, again?"

"Kelsey. Kelsey Garrett. I write for the *Country Caller Gazette*." She started to extend her hand, but stopped when she realized LilliFay wasn't listening.

"God told Moses to write the rules down so there'd be no mistakes. Told them point-blank it was a sin to kill someone else."

She paused, her voice definitely dimmed. "But didn't He also warn about coveting another woman? Why, yes, yes He did. Who's to say which sin is worse? No one can know the heart of a man, not really." With that, LilliFay lowered the book. Only then did Kelsey notice the woman's fingers were trembling. "I don't know what else to tell you right now. Go back to that newspaper of yours and write what you will. But I can't help you anymore." The Bible disappeared into the pocket of Lilli-Fay's apron, and she smoothed her hand over her hair. Her fingers definitely were trembling. "You're young. You'll learn. Believe me, you'll learn."

Those were LilliFay's final words to her, as she backed away and then left the room altogether. Kelsey had no choice but to find her way through the stranger's house, past the chorus of angels, away from the picture on the foyer table, all alone. When she walked out the front door, she paused on the landing and a moment later, LilliFay firmly clicked the deadbolt shut behind her.

The *Country Caller Gazette* anchored a strip center in the heart of Enterprise, one of only three such centers in town. The building—a one-story stucco with plate-glass windows—included an adjoining print shop, a taxidermy store, and the Grande Burrito, on the corner. Not much to look at, but then again, most people didn't visit the newsroom except to drop off a wedding announcement or place a classified ad for an unwanted refrigerator.

Kelsey parked in her usual spot after leaving Mrs. Holiday's house and swung open the driver's side door. Stepping from air conditioning onto hot asphalt was like walking into an invisible wall. Only this wall pressed against her chest and shoulders and followed her no matter where she turned, even though the sun would set soon on the horizon.

She reached for the door to the newsroom and swung it wide. Renee, her editor, didn't like surprises, and she'd hung a sleigh bell to the handle, which jangled when Kelsey entered.

A waist-high counter separated the foyer from the newsroom, and served as a landing pad for all sorts of paperwork. Times were tough, as they were for all newspapers, and they'd recently begun to include a free subscription with every classified ad. Of course, their distributors didn't have the most reliable aims, so lots of folks had grown accustomed to finding a newspaper on their front lawn whether they paid for a subscription or not.

Renee glanced up from her computer. Even though night would fall soon, Kelsey's editor was still hard at work.

Renee's desk faced one wall, while Kelsey's faced the other. Between them was a table for the sports reporter—a mishmash of dirty coffee mugs, gimme caps, and protein bars—and a desk used by the graphic artist. Ever since she'd had her third child, though, the artist worked from her home and performed her magic on their copy from twenty miles away.

All of which meant silence, blessed silence, on this early Friday evening. She could work in peace, even without the earplugs she kept stashed by her computer mouse. Kelsey dropped her purse to the ground and pulled out the piece of notebook paper she'd slid into her back pocket.

"Well?" Renee peered at her from around a monitor. A single gal, she let Kelsey know early on there were two things she wouldn't tolerate: dangling participles and unnamed sources.

"I didn't get much from the pastor's wife," Kelsey admitted. "Lady wanted to quote me the Bible, though." There, in a sea of blue, LilliFay had made a point of brandishing the Good Book like a weapon instead of saying something Kelsey could quote in her newspaper story. Either LilliFay was innocent of any crime, or she was terribly devious. "Maybe I'll try the police sergeant."

Renee nodded. "Hines will tell you what's up. Course, he might not know much at this point."

"How long's it take to get an autopsy report around here?"

"Could be a week or more, since it has to go up to Houston. They'll get a preliminary report, though, and that'll at least tell you the cause of death."

"Do you think the body's that of the missing girl?"

Renee looked at her askance. "Who else would it be? She goes missing on a Sunday, and they find a body three days later. No one leaves Enterprise without some kind of trail. Too many folks around here know each other."

"Well, then, did you know her?" Renee had been so tight-lipped about her neighbors that Kelsey assumed she was an insider, a lifelong resident like the rest of them.

"Do I look like I go to church?" Renee chuckled. "My church is a cup of coffee and the Sunday comics. So, no, I didn't know the girl who played piano at the church. Lots of folks did, though."

Kelsey settled into her chair and fired up the computer screen by typing in a password. If they would only confirm the identity of the murder victim, she'd have a starting point. With or without LilliFay Holiday, she'd have a springboard for the most exciting story to cross her desk since she first arrived in Enterprise. It sure beat trying to stretch the monthly meeting of the municipal utilities district into a front-page feature.

She easily found the website for the Enterprise Police Department, along with a telephone number for its sergeant. It was time to get answers so she could piece together a decent story and add some weight to the portfolio under her bed. As she lifted the telephone receiver, Renee called out to her.

"I'd go there, if I were you. You're bound to get more information in person."

Kelsey put the receiver back on the handset. Renee was right. While a phone interview might have worked when she was a student in Houston, where everyone was a stranger and no one thought twice about communicating that way, here in Enterprise things were different, she'd come to find. People didn't seem to trust the telephone as much as a visit, where they could speak face to face. And, email? It was much quicker to track someone down at the Enterprise High School football game on a Friday night. To be honest, it was a lot more fun, too.

She grabbed her purse from the floor. "You're right. The sergeant doesn't know me from Adam. Maybe if I pay him a visit I can get some answers."

Renee nodded. "Now you're thinking. If nothing else, you can read his face and find out how much he knows. Tell him I said 'hi,' will you?"

"Sure thing." Kelsey ducked around the counter and swatted at the sleigh bells as she left. "You know Christmas isn't for seven months." But Renee had returned to her work. Even though it was officially Friday night, her editor would still be at it for a few more hours. No wonder both of them were unmarried. Who would want to marry someone whose idea of a hot Friday night included the newspaper's style guide, a pile of press releases, and a story budget for the next day?

The minute Kelsey stepped out the newspaper's door, humidity settled onto her upper body. Even this late in the day, heat enveloped her like a wool blanket. She fired up her car—and its air conditioning—and drove down Fifth Street, one of the main arteries through town.

She turned right at the light and headed north for a few blocks. The Enterprise Police Department sat on the edge of town, mainly because they needed some acreage for the police cars and drunk tank. Made of cinder blocks, the building had been bomb-proofed, just in case. No windows, except for the front entrance, which had been filmed with a silverish lining, a beige polymer paint that did double duty and repelled mortar, and a separate outbuilding for the electrical system.

She swung into the parking lot, which was empty save for two police cruisers, and picked a spot near the front door. The coolness from the car's air conditioner disappeared within a second when she stepped onto hot concrete. No matter how many years she lived in southeast Texas—some twenty-nine at this point—she'd never get used to the summer heat. Made her wish she lived in Colorado, until fall would roll around and a slight breeze might blow in from the Gulf of Mexico.

She spotted the department's only female deputy as soon as she walked through the door. Earline was gray-haired and wiry, with not an ounce of fat on her. Kelsey couldn't imagine the woman chasing a criminal down an alley, or wrestling with a two-hundred-pound drunk. Then again, once Earline fixed that cold stare on someone, she probably didn't have to chase him.

"Evening." Earline walked to the front counter, her navy uniform made darker by the paleness of her skin.

"Hello." Kelsey extended her hand over the counter. "I'm here to see Sergeant Hines, if he's available."

Earline shook her hand with a steely grip. "He's here, but busy as all get-out. Who are you?"

Kelsey gulped. Maybe she'd been wrong about Earline's ability to wrestle a two-hundred-pound drunk. This one was tough. "I'm a reporter working on a story. I'll be quick, I promise."

Earline grunted and turned away, giving Kelsey a moment to look around the room, which was furnished entirely in metal. Silver chairs, pewter desks, nickel filing cabinets, all of them the color of old, scratched dimes. Everything looked clean, functional, and sparse. All except for a large oak desk placed in the back of the room, which commanded a position of authority. The oasis of oak had an enormous deer head over it, with glassy eyes that kept watch over the scene below, which included Sergeant Hines, seated behind the desk.

After a moment, Earline motioned for her to come to the back. Kelsey stepped around the front counter—just like the newsroom's, only this counter didn't have the jumble of papers and file folders that hers did—and approached the oak desk.

Sergeant Hines stood when she neared, his head almost touching the animal's chin. A good six-and-a-half-feet tall, he towered over both her and Earline, his burly frame outweighing theirs by at least a hundred pounds. White-haired, with thin wire glasses, he fit her image of a small-town sheriff to a T. All that was missing were the cowboy boots under the uniform, which she was certain would be there if only she checked.

"Have a seat, young lady." The sergeant fell back into his own chair once she settled onto a hard steel stool. She tried to ignore the glassy eyes watching her from above.

"Thank you for seeing me." While the rest of the police station looked spotless—each paperclip, police report, and file folder in place—the sergeant's desk was a mess. A cigarette ashtray overflowed with spent butts and a decade's worth of notes crested around the telephone. Good thing the desk was oversized, because there was no way a regulation office desk would fit the piles he had accumulated.

"Understand you're a reporter." The sergeant appraised her from behind his oval glasses.

"Yes, I write for the *Country Caller*. Been here only six months or so."

"I knew that." He waved his hand over the desk. "You were the talk of the town the first week or so. We all wondered how long you'd last, coming from Houston and all."

"Really?" She didn't know whether to feel flattered or appalled. Maybe a little of each, she decided. "I'm not that exciting, trust me. At least, not as exciting as what happened this afternoon. Where exactly did you find the body?"

The sergeant pushed the glasses higher on his nose. "We didn't find her. Some teenager did. Turns out he skipped school to do some fishing on the bayou, and there she was."

"What was the condition of the body?" She reached into her purse for the slim reporter's notebook that never left the front pocket, and flipped open the cover to the first page.

"Too soon to say anything to the press." He shrugged as if that should be that.

"Look, Sergeant . . . you and I both know whoever got there first knows exactly what happened to the body. Were there rope burns, knife wounds, anything like that?"

The sergeant clenched his jaw instead of answering. While she didn't want to anger him, she also didn't want to walk away empty-handed. Her job was to get the story, as much as she could at this early date, even if the details were sketchy. If she didn't get the facts out, gossip would soon fill in the holes for them.

"It won't help you to shut me down," she told him. "You're going to make it easier for people's imaginations to run wild. Next thing you know, the body will have machine gun tracks, and there'll be some lunatic gang member on the loose."

He must have realized she was right, because his face unclenched little by little. All the while, the mounted deer above her head cocked its antlers in permanent surprise.

"Suppose you're right." A thin smile appeared on his lips. "People may have been wrong about you. Said you'd never last. I think you're going to get on just fine."

The tension between them eased, just a bit, and she poised the pen over the notepad. "Okay, let's start again. You said a teenager found the body on the bayou. Where? And, at what time?"

"Call it the south side of town, about one o'clock."

"But the kid should have been in school. Wasn't he afraid to call you?"

"Not near as afraid as finding a dead girl at his feet. He was some knucklehead from the high school. We know his family . . . dad was a big-deal football player way-back-when. Playing hooky is the least of this kid's troubles." The trill of a telephone rang out, which she hoped he would ignore. No such luck. The policeman pointed to the phone, then to the reporter's notebook. "That's all we know at this point. No bullet holes from a machine gun, just a dead girl lying in some rye grass."

She flipped the notebook closed. At least she knew more now. Plus, the town's sergeant had tested her resolve, and, near as she could tell, she seemed to have passed his test.

Sergeant Hines leaned forward to grab the telephone, by now on its third ring. "One other thing. We've got a positive ID on the body. It was Becca Cooper, all right."

Kelsey's head jerked up. She was about to say more, but the sergeant had lifted the telephone to his ear. Clearly, their interview was over, though her questions had just begun.

CHAPTER 3

Reverend Holiday pulled into the church's parking lot, which was empty this late in the day, LilliFay's accusation still ringing in his ears. The minute he extinguished the engine, he laid his head against the steering wheel and forced himself to take several long, deep breaths.

In all the months he'd been with Becca Cooper, no one had ever caught him alone with her. Or so he had thought. Of course, the congregation had so many members, someone could have spotted them dashing from their cars to the front door of the church's lakeside condominium, but they always arrived at night, and they always traveled separately. Even if they were spotted, an onlooker would probably assume they were there for the same church retreat.

Second Coming Charismatic Church used the eight-bedroom condo for just about everything from family retreats to teenage summer camps. It was nothing special, just a two-story, walk-up condominium with a view of the lake, which he and Becca rarely saw because he was careful to close the drapes. But that always seemed fine with her. He couldn't exactly check them into a ritzy hotel and expect to remain anonymous. So his "dates" with Becca were always at the condominium. He always told himself it would be the last time. Kidding himself, really. Once they began, he couldn't stop even if he wanted to, and at that point he didn't want to.

They should have been more careful. He knew that now. He

had warned Becca a few months back he'd have to stop visiting the condo. She didn't take the news too kindly, but he knew that when she stopped to think about it, she'd agree with him. He needed all of his energy for the church, and the guilt was just about killing him.

But Becca had made their affair so easy. Because he couldn't give her much, she didn't expect much. A dinner here, some peonies there. Maybe a book about getting over the trauma of divorce. Why, that was the reason they had gotten together in the first place.

He always saw Becca on Sunday mornings, of course, though it was only her profile, a glimpse of her from behind the grand piano. Then, one day, Becca made an appointment with him for counseling. She couldn't get over the bad marriage she'd left behind.

He remembered the first time she walked into his office. She was so beautiful—with wheat-colored hair and full lips—and brimming with life. The strange thing was, she reminded him of LilliFay before they were married. Sweet, but strong.

He offered Becca several Bible verses to help with her pain and he prayed with her, a wonderful excuse for holding her hand with those long, musician's fingers and unpolished nails. He'd been under a lot of stress, going for nights on end without sleep, what with the traveling and problems in church. That first session with Becca, he could barely keep his eyes open. Then, gradually, he started to look forward to their weekly counseling sessions. No matter how rough his week had been, when he saw her name in his appointment book, he'd smile. Knowing she'd soon be in his office for a whole forty-five minutes, sitting across from him, speaking in her gentle voice about how hard she was trying to get over her failed marriage. He would give her a hug when she left, but it was a platonic hug, like a father might give his daughter. She didn't seem surprised. In fact, she leaned into him, reciprocating the embrace, each time for a split second longer.

Now this, he remembered perfectly. It was a Tuesday morning, three months after the start of their sessions, when they both agreed she seemed to be doing much better. And it struck him then that he couldn't count on his forty-five minutes of happiness any longer. Of course there were always Sunday mornings, but he could barely watch her from the corner of his eye. He would no longer read her name penciled in his secretary's—Velma's—calendar. He would no longer breathe in her perfume, a mix of lemon and cloves, and hear her laugh undulating like a musical scale. So he kissed her. Once, on the forehead. It was an innocent kiss, like a blessing. And, she didn't flinch. She didn't pull away, and she didn't seem shocked that a man in his position would place his lips against her skin. She giggled, which made his heart beat all the faster and let him hope beyond hope that this was not the end. Either he spoke next or she did, but they both agreed she would sign up for the upcoming scripture retreat that weekend, an annual event held at the condominium.

"Friday, then?" he'd asked.

"Of course," she had replied.

It wouldn't be easy, he knew. Everyone would want his attention and they'd all fawn over him, as if standing beside him somehow made them more special. But at least she'd be in the same building, close enough for him to hear her laugh and catch a whiff of lemon as she walked between the rooms. And, LilliFay had given up attending those church retreats years ago, so she wouldn't be a problem.

He purposefully ignored Becca all through the Friday night meeting. He spoke on Genesis, good and evil, and she sat in the back row. Their eyes met exactly twice, and exactly twice he lost his place and stumbled over his words. He knew what was coming. He knew their lives were going to change, but he also knew that if he didn't go through with this, something inside him would die. Already he moved from sermon to sermon on automatic, like a wind-up toy being forced to repeat the same words over and over. Speaking about things that only affected other people. Love. Passion. Sin. These were things that only affected other people.

He had been a virgin the night he married LilliFay. After he finished making love to her for the first time, LilliFay had looked at him in horror and asked if they ever had to do that again. By their fourth wedding anniversary, it was clear they would not have children, and they stopped sleeping together. Which seemed to suit both of them, because he didn't have the time or the energy, and she didn't seem interested. So they lived, kissing once in the morning and once at night, and she gradually got heavier and heavier and took to staying in the kitchen when he came home from a long trip away. She didn't even bother to greet him at the front door anymore. The worst part was, he didn't care.

He deserved better. He did the Lord's work all day, every day, with no thought for himself. Maybe that was all right in the beginning, but he wasn't going to live forever.

Fortunately, he knew the Bible very well, and he could come up with a reason for anything, even adultery. The Bible said to follow the commandments, but it also said that if you break one of them you've broken them all. Who hadn't invalidated his pledge never to sin?

He knew of a very famous pastor, divorced, who kept his pulpit and his paycheck even though he remarried a beauty half his age. Didn't the Bible prohibit a man from leaving his wife? So hadn't he earned the right to fall, just this once? To fall with Becca, with pure motives in his heart and no malice for anyone else?

He somehow managed to stumble through the talk he was giving to the small group of people sprawled around the condo living room, then he answered a few questions before leading them in closing prayer. He prayed for grace. When he opened his eyes, Becca had disappeared, the woven curtain in front of the sliding glass door wavering in the breeze. He followed her, shrugging off the hands that reached out to him. He was chasing after the smell of her. And there she was. She stood by the tennis court, a double court that backed up to a stand of trees, and she pressed her finger to her lips.

In an instant they had ducked behind the tennis court, enveloped by a curtain of branches. He kissed her fiercely, like a starving man invited to a banquet. She tasted like cinnamon gum. She didn't protest; she just fell with him softly to the ground. It was the best, and the worst, night of his life.

Now, sitting all alone in his car in the parking lot at the church, Bobby shuddered violently.

CHAPTER 4

After saying good-bye to Sergeant Hines and his deputy, Kelsey fired up her car in the police station parking lot, more determined than ever to follow up on the story. Since Becca Cooper had played piano at Second Coming Charismatic Church, that seemed as good a place as any to start.

She drove back to town deep in thought, a series of red-brick ranch houses passing by her windshield in a blur. So some teen-aged kid had skipped school that day, thinking he would do a little fishing on the bayou instead of sitting through another algebra lesson. Only he got more than he bargained for when his biggest catch of the day turned out to be a woman's body, tucked among the reeds and wildflowers that normally bordered the bayou's waters. And that body was none other than the accompanist at the largest church—and some would say the only church that mattered—in Enterprise.

She finally noticed her surroundings the closer she got to town. Enterprise seemed to have a lock on large spreads of land anchored by sprawling ranch houses that sprouted like pin oaks from the soil. Neat and tidy, most homesteads included a few outbuildings, a flagpole that held both the American and Texas flags, and the obligatory wooden doghouse for a family's hunting dogs. Add a chain-link fence around the property and a pickup truck or two, and that was the average house in town.

The best part of Enterprise was the wide-open view: no billboards, or skyscrapers, no cellular towers to block it. Just mile after mile of flat roads and thick trees, some several hundred years old. Time ran slowly here, as slowly as the stream that flowed around the perimeter of the city.

She arrived at the parking lot of Second Coming Charismatic Church in no time at all. Since it was after dinner, only a few cars remained in the lot, including a mammoth luxury sedan anchored in a parking space reserved for the Senior Pastor.

Kelsey drove into the lot and pulled alongside the pastor's car. As soon as she bolted from the car, curiosity got the better of her and she peered into the darkened sedan. It was impeccable, empty save for a potted peony and some sheet music. Odd, wasn't it?

She sidestepped the sedan and hopped onto a cracked curb that led to the sanctuary. The blistering heat had mellowed, tempered by a slight breeze. In front of her lay double-wide doors that signaled the sanctuary, but more intriguing was a sign that pointed toward the church's administrative offices.

Which seemed about as good a place as any to start. She didn't have a plan other than to visit the place Becca Cooper had last worked, and talk to the people who knew her.

The minute she entered the administrative offices, she smelled air freshener and disinfectant. A kelly-green carpet rolled down the hall like a blanket of grass, and the walls were painted virginal white.

It looked like everyone had already called it a day. She strode through the empty hall—her fingers around a pen nestled in her khakis—until gradually, she heard a voice. Two voices, really. The words overlapped, but she heard a deep baritone, followed by a softer, feminine tone.

An imposing mahogany door featured a sign that read Senior Pastor's Office. Lured by a sound, Kelsey pressed her hand against the cool wood, the hair on her forearms bristling. She checked left, then right, and laid her ear against the door.

"What would you have me do, Velma? I can't keep quiet forever."

Odds were good the voice belonged to Reverend Holiday. Deep and rich, such a voice would captivate an auditorium full of people. It rose and fell with the cadence of a hypnotist.

The female spoke next, very softly. "Anything but this. They're goin' to think you had something to do with it, Reverend. I won't let that happen." She must have marshaled her courage, because her voice rose on the final word.

Kelsey leaned even closer to the door. This wasn't what she expected, but then again, that's how most good stories developed.

"You're not going to go behind the pulpit and confess your sins," the woman continued. "It's too late. Don't you see that? It's too late."

"I owe it to them, Velma. They believe in me."

At that, something rustled behind the door. Before she had a chance to retreat, it swung open and Kelsey tumbled into the office. Frantically, she reached for a side table and gripped the edge of it. There she stood, staring up at two faces that looked as shocked to see her as she felt at the moment.

She'd been right. The baritone belonged to Reverend Holiday. She recognized his face from the picture in LilliFay's foyer. Only the picture didn't do him justice. In person he was much more handsome. Broad-shouldered, a touch of gray at his temples, and smooth, tanned skin. His partner was a good two feet shorter and a hundred pounds lighter; a diminutive woman who wore a prim gray bun. The woman glared at Kelsey, clearly unamused by this turn of events.

"We're closed for the day, honey," she said. "You'll have to come back."

"I'm . . . I'm sorry," Kelsey stammered by way of apology. "I must have gotten lost. I left something here and I'm trying to find it."

The hard cast of the reverend's face softened. "We have a lost and found closet, but you're in the wrong hall. Come with me and I'll show you the way."

The woman turned on the reverend. "We're not done here! I'm sure she can find it herself."

Whatever it was they were discussing, the man seemed only too happy to leave it behind. "Nonsense," he said. "We can finish our discussion later."

The woman snorted, then pivoted on her heel. "Don't do it," she whispered to the reverend before walking out. She grazed Kelsey with her elbow, but didn't bother to turn around.

When the woman—apparently Velma—disappeared into the hall, Kelsey faced the formidable Reverend Holiday.

"I'm sorry. I didn't mean to interrupt. Maybe I should just leave."

"No, it's all right. You're not that far off. I can see how you might get turned around in this place." The reverend touched her shoulder gently. "You must be new. I don't recognize you."

There was no time like the present. Now that she had Becca Cooper's employer alone, it seemed as good a time as any to find out what the man knew. "I'll be truthful, Reverend. I'm not looking for the lost and found. I write for the local newspaper, and I'd like to ask you about Becca Cooper."

Clearly, her words stunned him, because he furrowed his brow, as if he didn't quite understand. "Excuse me?"

"I'm here to ask you about someone. Becca Cooper. You knew her, right?"

He stared at the pretty woman in front of him, unsure of what to do next. Every minute of this day, a new surprise had reached up and slapped him. First, the conversation with LilliFay. Finding out she'd known about Becca Cooper all along, biding her time, staying silent. Then, to be cornered by Velma—his faithful employee of thirty years—in his own office yet. Just one more affront to his position at the church. And now this.

"Of course." He turned away from the stranger, drawn to the familiar leather armchair tucked into the kneehole of his writing desk. He sat down and appraised the desk's surface before speaking. His favorite pen lay next to a pad of yellow legal paper. He always sketched out his sermons in permanent ink. Hard to imagine a new student coming out of seminary doing that. "What can I do for you?"

"When did you last see Becca Cooper?" she asked him, point blank.

Confidence, he liked that. Obviously, this girl wasn't afraid of him. Pretty, she was, with auburn hair, chin-length, and large brown eyes. She didn't look like she could harm him in any way, but then again, they never did.

"I really don't recall." No, he had faced much worse enemies than this. Why, he had faced the devil himself. It had happened once, a long time ago, in a shantytown in Jamaica. He thought back to the island and the throng of villagers who escorted him to a simple reed hut. Where he held a cross over a woman possessed by a demon and prayed over her for eight hours straight. When he had finished, drenched in sweat, the person lay uncoiled at his feet, while the family's dog lay twisted in pain. No, he'd faced much worse foes than this. Why, he'd faced the devil himself.

"My dear, just what do you want to know?" He leaned back against the cool leather amid his trusty bookcase, the *Dictionary of Famous Quotations*, the boxes of tissue paper scattered around the room.

"Miss Cooper worked here, right? She left her home in Oklahoma to take a job at your church."

Reverend Holiday nodded. Forthrightness. He liked that. This woman asked tough questions and wanted answers. He could respect that, actually. He just wasn't going to play along. "Do you go to church, child?"

"Huh?" The reporter looked puzzled, as if no one had ever asked her *that* question before.

Reverend Holiday clasped his hands. He sat on the edge of the armchair now, ready to do battle. "I asked you if you went to church."

"Used to. But that's beside the point. I'm asking you the questions." The girl withdrew a ballpoint pen from the pocket of her slacks.

"I see. Well, child—may I call you that?" Without waiting for an answer, he continued. "If you're not attending church regularly, you're not feeding your soul."

The reporter clicked at her pen. "Reverend, I came here to ask you about Becca Cooper. Not about whether I go to church."

Reverend Holiday rose. Maybe it was better to stand above your enemy. "She was my employee, yes. Now, why don't you join us—"

"When did you find out she was missing?"

This girl wasn't about to be swayed. He reached for a maroon book lying on his desk. If she wanted to play hardball with him, he could take it. Only he'd serve it right back to her. "Here at Second Coming, we rely on the word of God."

The reporter looked pained, as she struggled to control something she couldn't control. "But the missing—"

"Our church goes back fifty years. It's a fine church, child. Services are at nine-thirty and eleven o'clock. We'd love to have you come worship with us on Sunday." He looked straight into her eyes, unafraid. Why, he'd faced the devil himself.

The reporter crossed her arms, seeming to forget all about the ballpoint pen she'd brought. "Fine, if you're not going to answer my questions—"

"By the way, we also have services Sunday night every week, six o'clock." He smiled benignly. He had spent thirty years in the pulpit, and he had thousands of souls in his corner. What was one reporter, when he'd stared at the face of the devil?

"She's dead, Reverend."

The ground shifted beneath him, plain as day. It actually moved beneath his feet, if that was possible. "What did you say?"

"They found her body on the bayou today. She's dead."

He watched the stranger's lips move, saw the tilt of her head as she spoke. But her words held no weight; they floated end-over-end in the air. It couldn't be true. It wasn't true. A perfect stranger couldn't be telling him they'd found Becca Cooper's body. It was impossible. Wasn't it?

Kelsey turned to leave, mortified she'd blurted out the truth so harshly. Normally, she could control her temper better than that. But she hated being placated, and that was exactly what the reverend had been doing. Treating her like a child: a naïve, easily dismissed child. She'd had no choice but to tell him what she knew, even if it did kill any chance the conversation would continue.

What could she do? The reverend had collapsed into his leather armchair, one hand on his chest and the second clinging to his Bible for dear life. Obviously, her news had shocked him . . . that much was clear. But which part? The part about Becca Cooper being dead? The fact they'd found her floating in the shallow waters of the bayou on a quiet Friday afternoon? Or the part where a reporter delivered the news, which meant a whole lot of people would soon hear the same announcement?

"Are you all right, Reverend?"

He stared straight ahead, unblinking. She had no choice but

to back out of the office, little by little. *So much different from her earlier, dramatic entrance.* She retraced her steps gingerly. She hadn't gotten much from their conversation, other than to find out he was surprised by the discovery of Becca Cooper's body. Granted, the man was beside himself at this point, but he hadn't even asked *how* the young woman had died.

She retraced her steps out of the office, then down the church's hallway. As she passed the sanctuary, she glimpsed the back of another man, this one leaning over a pew, focused on some task or another. Not wanting to disturb him, she tiptoed past the open door. The stranger must have heard her, though, because he turned as she passed. Tall and muscular, he held a hammer in one hand and a nail in the other. A leather tool-belt was slung low on his hips.

"Evenin'," the stranger said as she passed. The voice was gentle and well-mannered.

"Hello," she replied, taking in the white t-shirt, the shock of sun-bleached hair. A lock of it fell into his eyes when he nodded. Beautiful eyes, really. Pale aqua, rimmed in an even darker blue. She guessed they were both the same age . . . twenty-nine or so.

"Can I help you?"

"No, I'm just on my way out."

He put the hammer in his tool belt, pulled off a leather glove, and offered her his hand. A light cloud of dust floated between them. "Name's Park."

"Nice to meet you, Park." His hand felt warm against her palm. "I just saw Reverend Holiday. You might want to check on him."

The good-looking stranger cocked his head. "Is that right?"

"I had some bad news for him. I was a little worried about him when I left." Suddenly she felt shy under his gaze and withdrew her hand.

"I'll do that. You a member here?"

"No, I'm a reporter. From over at the *Enterprise Country Caller.*"

His eyes lit up. "You're that new reporter who moved in a few months back. Heard all about you."

"Really? Me?"

He chuckled. "Not a whole lot happens in Enterprise without folks hearing about it. Let's see. You graduated from the university in Houston, you're a single gal, not too friendly, from what I've heard."

"Now wait a minute . . ." she began to protest, but his grin stopped her cold. "All right, maybe I *have* been working a lot. I don't have much time to get out. But what do you folks do . . . print up a bio on someone when she gets to town?"

The smile remained. Deep creases lined his tanned face, which was better suited for the wild outdoors than any whitewashed hall. "Pretty much. Oh, and you're renting the Riley cottage. Folks give you a year or two, then say you'll hightail it back to Houston."

"I like it there," she insisted. "Lots of quiet and lots of privacy. Or so I thought. How long have you worked here?"

He ran his hand along the back of the pew, caressing it. His left hand was bare, with nails chewed short. "I don't work here. I volunteer to keep the place nice. Any time they have somethin' that needs fixing, I'm their man." He pointed at the glossy back of a pew in front of him. "See these pews? Hand-carved walnut. Worked 'em myself. Every once in a while, I can't help but come in here and tinker."

"I can see that." She took a step back. All this time she'd forgotten about the real reason she'd come to the church. Of course, she could always blame it on the man's rugged face or his gentle twang. "Say, did you know anything about Becca Cooper, the pianist here?"

His smile faded for the first time, and he sucked in his lower lip before answering. "Great gal. Gifted, too. She had a way with the piano you wouldn't believe."

Immediately, Kelsey noticed he used the past tense. "So what do you know about her? You know she went missing?"

The man lowered his eyes. "Yeah, I'd heard. Hard to believe she's actually gone." When he glanced up again, those eyes were defiant. "Why, what'd you hear?"

She'd already shocked one person on this visit and didn't want to repeat that scene. Better for him to learn about Becca Cooper's death from someone else. If she didn't watch it, people all over town would start to avoid her, as if she were the harbinger of death. That couldn't happen if she hoped to learn anything at all about the young woman's murder. "Nothing. It's just sad, that's all. Well, I've got to get going. Nice to meet you."

She stuck out her hand, but he didn't return the gesture. In his left hand, though, the man still gripped a nail and his grip must have tightened, because the skin had blanched pure white.

CHAPTER 5

Saturday morning dawned hot and bright. LilliFay walked along the dusty bayou, a cluster of daisies in her hand. It'd been years since she'd walked this path, years since she'd come here to learn the lay of the land.

She knew the best way to discover a place was to get lost in it, which didn't make a whole lot of sense to Bobby, him being so orderly and all. Why, she could have spent hours wandering along the dirt paths that meandered up and down the bayous of Enterprise, while Bobby would've been sick at wasting time in such a frivolous manner. It didn't seem so frivolous now, seeing as how she could make an educated guess as to where Becca Cooper's body had been found.

A hiss rose from the reeds; the buzzing of cicadas. They reminded her of an incoming airplane, soft at first, then growing loud. Unlike a lot of people in town, she liked the hot, humid air that made everything here grow so green and pretty, especially in May, when wildflowers splayed across the dirt. Their pastel blooms couldn't compete with the garish color ahead, though. The police had strung harsh yellow crime scene tape across two sawhorses in the distance. She knew enough from watching crime shows on TV that the police had created a barricade with plastic caution tape to mark the spot where Becca's body had been found.

She approached the area with reverence. So final to see tape stretched thin from one sawhorse to another. Of course, everything on the bayou was wispy, and Sergeant Hines probably had no choice but to create his own mooring for the tape. She could read the caution warning clear as day. Her grip felt sweaty against the flowers, whether from nerves or humidity it was hard to say.

Someone had trampled a path from the walkway to the stream. Probably when they dragged Becca's body. But today, LilliFay was the only person on the bayou, the only person to see where the tracks had flattened a hill of fire ants to pieces, the only person to listen for when the cicadas paused.

She yanked apart the daises she'd brought and dropped the first one over the crime scene tape and onto hard-packed ground. The sound of her heart matched the swish of the flower as it plinked to the ground. Such a pity. How a young girl's life had ended so tragically, though her demise wasn't totally undeserved.

She didn't want to believe stories about Becca and Bobby the first time around. When Harris, one of the church's most upright deacons, suggested something was amiss, she chalked it up to idle gossip. Why, even Harris wasn't perfect. Didn't his own grandson blurt out right there in the middle of Sunday School that his pappy liked to cuss out salespeople who dared call his house at dinnertime? That little boy knew words no child should be privileged to know, thanks to his upstanding granddaddy.

But when Velma started to drop the very same hints, LilliFay couldn't look the other way any longer. She had to attend the upcoming scripture retreat, even though it took place on a Friday night, not on a Thursday, which was when Velma said she normally covered for them.

Her mind reeled back to that night as she dropped another daisy over the tape. She chose to drive herself to the retreat, without telling a single soul about her plans. If Bobby knew, nothing would happen between him and Becca that night, and she'd still be left to wonder why people insisted on torturing her with rumors and innuendo. She didn't suspect much was wrong until she pulled into the condo complex's parking lot and saw Bobby's beloved sedan right across from Becca's convertible, plain as day.

Course, the woman had every right to attend the scripture retreat, same as anyone else. It didn't mean anything untoward was going on. LilliFay almost turned back at that point, ashamed for her sinful thoughts, ready to take Bobby's word for it that nothing had changed between them. The glances she saw pass between him and Becca on Sunday morning were just a product of her overactive imagination. Probably it was the devil who was planting such sinful thoughts. Now that Second Coming was prospering, it probably angered him to see the heathens finally get some religion.

By the time she arrived in the parking lot at the condo that night, the sermon must have ended, because the sliding glass door stood ajar. She watched a figure slip through the door and glide toward the tennis courts.

Everything slowed at that point, she remembered. Every detail stood apart, distinct, unmistakable. A soft breeze blew when she rolled down her car window. Moonshine exposed a head of golden hair. A second figure slid from behind the wavering curtain and rushed to join Becca by the tennis court. Ran, really. Grasping for her. It was Bobby, taking Becca in his arms. Falling to the ground. LilliFay cried out at that point, a horrible, animal sound that gurgled in her throat and poured from her mouth. Course, no one heard her. They couldn't have heard her over the sound of two bodies falling to the ground.

She stayed in that car, frozen, for an hour. Watched as the shadowy figures finished what they had come for and wobbled to their feet. It must have been over quickly, because the moon only emerged one more time, but it seemed to last for days. She watched it all, awash in shame. Why would he do that with another woman? What did he hope to gain? She didn't understand, she couldn't understand, and she drove home that night in a trance that didn't break until her car reached the driveway, and she was safe again.

Now, watching a daisy fall to the ground, shame flowed through her all over again. Obviously, she had her flaws, otherwise this wouldn't have happened. None of this had to have happened; it could have turned out so much differently.

The flowers were gone now. LilliFay turned away from the wisp of reeds, the trampled ant hill, the telltale path of flattened grass by the stream's edge. Turned her back on all of it, every bit of it. What was done was done, Daddy used to say, and there was no going back. Even if she wanted to. And, she wasn't sure she wanted to.

Kelsey flung open the door to the Enterprise Police Department, nearly empty this early on a Saturday. Most people were at the weekly farmer's market on Fifth Street, buying cantaloupes and band booster t-shirts and pinwheels for their front yards. In fact, the police department's lone bicycle, which normally leaned against a far wall in the foyer, was gone. No doubt one of the town's three officers had planned to cruise through the stalls, card tables, and barbecue tents.

She paused in the lobby, a vestibule of sorts, which had blurry posters of child kidnappers and check forgers hanging on the walls. She also saw Sergeant Hines, still talking into the fat black telephone, his desk still awash in file folders and notebooks.

"Hello, Miss Garrett." It was Earline, same as yesterday.

"May I speak with Sergeant Hines?"

"Sure thing. Just a second." Earline shuffled toward the back, whispered something to Sergeant Hines, and retired to her own desk. When the police sergeant saw Kelsey, he hung up the telephone and moved forward.

"Morning, Miss Garrett." He nodded his head briskly, all business.

"I'm still working on the story, Sergeant. Do you have a minute?"

"Sure, come on back." He escorted her to the oak desk and waved once again to the battered stool in front of it. She took in the empty potato chip bags and gum wrappers on the desk, the sludgy cups of coffee, half-finished, and the month's worth of folders to file. It would be a wonder he could find anything. She also noticed something she hadn't before: a calendar thumb-tacked to the wall behind him, next to the mounted buck. Red tick marks crossed off most of the days.

"Thank you." She settled onto the stool. "I've been interview-ing folks about Becca Cooper. The pastor seems devastated by her death. His wife doesn't, though. Course the rumor mill says the good reverend was seeing the girl on the side."

"You're moving too fast, Miss Garrett. The investigation only started yesterday."

"I know that. I have to find out the truth." She withdrew her trusty notebook from the pocket of her purse. She swore that one day they'd have to surgically remove it from her hand. "Can you tell me the condition of the body? Do you know if she'd been dumped, or killed at the site?"

"From what we can tell, she'd been killed at the site. There were cast-off blood stains and the area had been disturbed."

"A teenager found the corpse, right?"

"Some kid named Shawn Deschamps. His father owns Midway Liquors. But you can't put that in . . . he's a minor. He's also trouble, but that's another story."

"No problem. So you think the victim was killed sometime

Friday morning?"

"That's what we figure. By the time the kid found her, rigor mortis had set in, so we know it happened at least three hours before he found her. Responding deputy said it looked like death by blunt trauma. The left side of her head had been bashed in."

Kelsey feverishly scribbled down notes as he spoke. If he was in the mood to talk, she was in the mood to listen. "So she was bludgeoned to death?"

It took him a moment to respond. "You know, we should wait for the autopsy report. Lucky for you, I was a homicide detective in my younger days, so they're letting me ride herd on this one. They're only sending down some detectives from Houston to corroborate what I find."

She glanced at the wall behind his head as he spoke, and saw again the ragged calendar. The red tick marks stopped at the end of the month. She'd heard from Renee that Sergeant Hines was long past retirement age, but he was too stubborn to pack it in. "Are you going somewhere?"

His eyes followed hers to the wall. "Oh, those? I'm counting off my days. Figure it's about time I take that pension. This isn't exactly how I wanted to end my career. A young woman dead, dumped in the bayou like garbage."

"I can imagine." She closed the notebook and laid it in her lap. "Let's talk off the record, then. Just you and me. Something else is bothering you, isn't it, Sergeant?"

He took a deep breath, then slowly exhaled. "She was pregnant, Miss Garrett. About four months along. Go ahead and put that in your story. Some son of a bitch murdered a pregnant lady."

"Oh, my." Kelsey paused, her mind awhirl. "How do you know it wasn't a woman who killed her?"

"Could be. We'll know more when we get the coroner's

report. Give me a few days. Keep in mind that everything's just speculation at this point."

She rose to leave. "Thank you. You've been very helpful. Good luck with the investigation and with your retirement when it comes up."

"Oh, we'll figure this out before then. I couldn't sleep good knowing there's a murderer somewhere in town." Deep furrows lined his forehead now. "What kind of person murders a pregnant gal?"

The door to the newsroom was locked when Kelsey arrived there, which meant that Renee had decided to cover a story of her own this Saturday morning. Most of the time, Renee stayed tethered to her computer, editing other people's work, but every now and again she couldn't resist working up her own story with her own byline. Said something about taking the editor out of the newsroom, but not the news out of the editor.

The sleigh bells heralded Kelsey's arrival. She approached Saturday mornings like any other day. In fact, sometimes Saturdays were the busiest workday of all, because people would wander in and out of the newsroom with band booster ads, pictures of newborns for the lifestyle section, and handwritten letters to the editor. Truth be told, she didn't mind coming in to work on the weekend since there wasn't much to be done around the cottage, other than to straighten up a bit and work on her portfolio. Better to make herself useful.

She dropped her purse to the floor and fired up her computer. Now that she had a few more details about Becca Cooper's death, thanks to Sergeant Hines, she'd start in on a feature story for Tuesday's edition. While the rest of the town trolled the farmer's market, rooted for a mud-splattered goalie on the soccer field, or eyed a whirl of pink at Miss Katy's School of Dance, she'd troll cyberspace for more information. Amazing what could be learned with just a few, well-placed keystrokes.

She tucked in her head and began to search for references to Becca Cooper of Enterprise, Texas, on her computer. Several mentions came up under that name, but all in the same breath as Second Coming Charismatic Church. A Yuletide Spectacular in the winter of '08, a music camp the summer before. Even a mention of her playing for a famous evangelist on one of his last swings through town.

As she trolled down the screen, one hit stopped Kelsey cold. It was a link to the *Caller's* own website, when it first appeared a few years before. Seems Becca Cooper of Enterprise had participated in an air show, of all things. From what Sergeant Hines had told her earlier, it would have been when the girl first arrived in town, fresh off an airplane from Broken Arrow.

Kelsey clicked on the link and the *Caller's* archives appeared. It looked like the reference was a cutline from a feature photo. Becca Cooper stood on the wing of a classic biplane, waving to the camera. Her blond hair flew straight back from her face, her mouth a broad smile. Standing behind her was none other than the good-looking man Kelsey had met at the church the night before. Name was Park, or something like that.

My, but they looked cozy. The man's arm was draped around the girl's waist, tight, by the way the fabric bunched around the woman's stomach. They looked downright ecstatic, like they belonged in an ad for a matchmaking service or an engagement ring store. Yes, his name was Park, all right. According to the cutline, Park Daniels had displayed his classic biplane with the help of one Becca Cooper, aged twenty-four.

Kelsey paused, while the computer screen waited for her next command. She typed in a string of words to call up any Becca Coopers of Broken Arrow, Oklahoma. Sure enough, fifteen hits popped up, most of them linked to a small community news-paper. It was one she'd never heard of.

She waited while the first site unscrolled on the screen. Mid-morning sun glared through the newsroom's window, testifying to another hot summer day. Good thing she'd left the air conditioning on back at the cottage. The last time she tried to save money and extinguish it before she left, a tub of butter sitting on her kitchen counter had melted all over the countertop.

Finally, the website finished downloading to her computer. The story explained that a man had been sentenced to six months' probation for attacking his estranged wife, Becca Cooper, of Broken Arrow, Oklahoma. A mug shot appeared in the right corner, which showed a disheveled man grimacing into the camera, his front teeth yellowed. Apparently, the husband had attacked his wife with a two-by-four he found in their garage, sending her to the hospital with a nasty concussion and enough witnesses to send him to jail. The story didn't explain what provoked the attack, but it did mention this was the third time police had been called to the young couple's apartment.

Interesting. All of this time she had assumed Becca Cooper left her hometown to take a more challenging job in Texas, not to escape an abusive husband who had sent her to intensive care with a nasty head wound.

The Oklahoma paper mentioned her husband received six months of jail time and a year of probation for the attack. But that was four years ago. Who knew where he was now, or if he had ever tried to contact Becca Cooper again?

Sleigh bells jangled against plate glass. Renee had returned to the office, her face flush with happiness.

"Man, I love being out there." She swung around the counter and plopped into her chair. Half-moons of sweat lined the arms of her t-shirt, but she didn't seem to mind.

"So, you got to cover something good?" Kelsey asked.

"Hardly. Unless you call an emergency meeting of the school board exciting. Seems next year's science textbook is the big debate right now." Renee fanned herself with her hand as she spoke. "But I love playing reporter again."

"Welcome to my world." The computer screen wavered in front of her, reminding her of her search. "Hey . . . I learned something interesting this morning. That body they found yesterday? It *was* Becca Cooper. Not only that, Sergeant Hines told me she was four months pregnant."

Renee stopped waving her hand. "You're kidding! That's something to put into your story."

"Wish I had more, though." After all, the police had yet to take anyone into custody and the exact cause of death was undetermined. "The body was found by some high school kid. Hines pretty much said he's a troublemaker. Son of the guy who owns Midway Liquors."

"He must mean Shawn. Yeah, Hines is right about that one."

"Turns out the kid ditched school yesterday to hang out on the bayou. Only he found a dead body by mistake. Think I should talk to him?"

Renee fell silent. Whenever she wanted Kelsey to make a decision about something, she'd take forever to respond. It was her way of forcing Kelsey to make a choice, which was irritating, but it worked.

"All right, I get it." As Renee liked to tell her, one day she'd be out there on her own, with no editor to watch her back, and then where would she be? "I'll go talk to him. Shouldn't take long. High school kids don't have much to say to anyone over sixteen." Kelsey smirked at her own joke and snatched her purse from the ground. "I feel like a yo-yo today. I've already been to the police station and back, and it's only ten o'clock."

No telling whether the boy would be at his father's business, but it was worth a shot. She waved to Renee, eased open the door to silence the bells, and ducked outside. Immediately, she squinted against the sun and made her way—half-blind—to her car.

Who knew where this day would end up? That was one of the best parts about being a reporter. Anything could happen between sunup and sundown. Sometimes the days with the least amount of planning turned out to be the best ones, especially now that another "person of interest" had been added to the mix.

CHAPTER 6

Kelsey sped away from the parking lot and cruised through town until she reached a different strip mall, this one on the west end. It was identical to hers, only it housed a liquor store on its corner, not the Grande Burrito.

She pulled up to the center, parked, and swung open the driver's side door. A neon sign hiccupped in the front window, barely visible in the bright sunlight. When she entered the cool, dim space, she first passed a metal rack of snack cakes, mini doughnuts, and potato chips. Garish banners hung from cheap foam ceiling tiles overhead: Longhorn Beer for the Lone Star State. Choose the Best, Forget the Rest. Play the Lottery! Eye-popping ads decorated the ceiling, the shelves, the walls. It seemed that every inch advertised liquor, cigarettes, or the Powerball lottery.

In the corner, a stand-up fan blew straggles of plastic tied to its blades, and a teenager slouched against the counter, his eyes glued to a magazine.

"Are you Shawn?" The boy had vampire-black hair that fell in his eyes, bad skin, and the delicate build of a young girl.

He slapped the x-rated magazine closed. "Yes, ma'am." Finally, he straightened, perhaps because she'd called him by name.

"I'm Kelsey Garrett, from the *Enterprise Country Caller.*" She stuck out her hand, which he stared at, nonplussed. "Can I talk to you?"

The boy shrugged. "Not like we're busy or anything." He peered at her from behind the lock of hair. While most kids in town wore letterman jackets and boot-cut jeans, this one sported a skull and crossbones on his long-sleeved t-shirt and his fingernails had been painted black.

"Sergeant Hines told me you found a body yesterday, on the bayou."

"Oh, man." He tugged the t-shirt sleeves higher. A small tattoo of a skull appeared above his wrist. "That was wicked."

"Did you know who it was?" Odds were good he had no idea. First off, he seemed the type to sleep until noon on Sundays, not go to any church. Plus, the murdered girl was ancient because she was at least twenty-eight or so.

"Course, I knew who it was." His eyes widened. They were bright and clear. "She gave me my first piano lesson." He shook his head, but the lock of hair remained firmly in place. "Got my ass kicked all through junior high for playing the piano, but it was worth it."

Kelsey blinked. The average teenaged boy in Enterprise was busy running blocking patterns on the football field come Saturday morning, not sitting on a piano bench running scales. This kid definitely *was* different.

"When did you stop taking lessons from her?" She glanced behind her, but there was nothing to sit on, so she leaned against the counter instead. Thankfully, they were the only two people in the store and probably in the entire strip center, for that matter.

"Freshman year." He rubbed the skull tattoo with his thumb. "Got tired of it. Figured I might as well take up the drums so my old man would get off my back."

Probably a wise decision. If dad was a former jock, he'd be more impressed with the high school drumline than a concert piano. "Do you have any idea what happened?"

He stopped rubbing his thumb for a moment. "No idea. I did my part by calling the cops."

At that moment, a figure walked through the door. It was a clean-cut man with a cowboy hat and a beer belly. "Who's your friend, son? You're not a truant officer, I hope. Shawn promised his mom and me he'll stay out of trouble till the end of school. Isn't that right?"

Shawn slid the magazine off the counter with his elbow, letting it drop to the floor undetected by his father. "That's right, sir. No trouble for a whole month."

"I'm not a truant officer." She glanced from the boy to his father. They shared nothing in common, save for the same clear, bright eyes. Sergeant Hines had been right, though. Even though his high school playing days must have been twenty years in the past, the elder Deschamps had the squat, muscular build of a defensive lineman. She pointed to a pack of gum in the display case. "I'll take that."

As she dug in her purse for change, Mr. Deschamps passed behind her, then joined his son at the cash register. "I don't recognize you. Are you new to town?"

"I work over at the newspaper. Been here about six months." She opened the pack of gum and offered it to both of them. "Came to find out what happened yesterday."

The elder Deschamps accepted a square of gum and popped it into his mouth. She could only imagine what he'd said when his progeny came home and said he'd found a dead girl on the bayou. "Shawn here told me he almost tripped over her. She plumb near matched the grass with that blond hair of hers."

"I don't know what I'd do if that happened to me," Kelsey said. "It's something you hear about in places like New York City or New Orleans, not in Enterprise."

"People didn't believe me back at school." Finally, Shawn had found a reason to rejoin the conversation. He seemed relieved now to be telling her what had happened. "They thought I made the whole thing up. Man, that would be twisted."

"Sergeant Hines said there are only a few people they're considering as suspects." Kelsey took off her gum's wrapper and folded the shiny square in two. "Reverend Holiday, of course." She glanced up to gauge the reaction of her words on the elder Deschamps, but his face remained blank. In fact, he seemed to be running through his own mental calculations, because he ground his gum purposefully against his molars. "And, his wife," Kelsey added.

"Mrs. Holiday's not so bad." Shawn glanced at her from behind the shock of hair. "For an old lady and all. She cracks me up with those hats."

Kelsey leaned across the counter even more. Luckily, there was nothing to interrupt the conversation, only the hum of the fan blowing the breeze around. Behind Shawn's head, cartons of cigarettes and cigarillos shared space in a locked cabinet, and a video camera duct-taped to the ceiling watched their every move. "There must be other suspects, though. I know she had an ex-husband in Oklahoma. Maybe he came back to town."

The father abruptly stopped chewing. "Great guy he turned out to be. If he ever showed up in town, there'd be a whole boatload of people waiting to greet him. Them and their shotguns, that is."

"So you knew she'd been abused when she came to town?"

"Hard to miss. She had a big ol' bruise by her eye. We thought she'd been in a car accident or something."

"I knew what happened." Shawn shot his father a knowing look from behind the shock of black hair. "That first lesson, I asked her how come her face was swollen up like that. She said she'd left a bad scene back home. The jerk popped her with a board."

"I'll tell you who they ought to look at." When Mr. Des-

champs resumed chewing, the movement was slow and deliberate. "They ought to look at Reverend Holiday's secretary. She's
the one had a vendetta against Becca Cooper."

"She's a frail old lady," Kelsey said. "Can't imagine she'd
have the strength to do something like this."

Mr. Deschamps burst out laughing. "Old Velma Wainwright?
Don't you believe it. That woman's strong as an ox and twice as
mean."

"You're kidding, right? She has to be seventy years old. What
could she do to someone like Becca Cooper?"

"I'll tell you what she could do." The man hooked his thumb
over his belt buckle and let his fingers rest against his blue
jeans. It was the biggest belt buckle she'd ever seen: shiny silver,
the size of a saucer, with a bucking horse and an elaborate
scrolled banner. "Junior here used to go to those summer camps
at the church. Think they call 'em Vacation Bible Schools. Old
Velma used to teach at the camps, until the parents got wind of
how she'd discipline the young'uns."

While the man's body relaxed, his lips were pursed, as if the
memory still left a bitter taste in his mouth, after all of these
years. "She'd make 'em sit on their hands until the poor kids'
fingers would fall asleep. Then, she'd smash their knuckles with
a stapler so they wouldn't feel it until their fingers started to
swell up. She was a mean old cuss, wasn't she, son?" She noticed
Shawn's eyes were glued to the countertop. So it was Shawn his
father was talking about.

"She's got a cruel streak, that woman," he continued. Mr.
Deschamps angled his body toward his son, which was probably
as close as the two of them ever got to touching. "I wouldn't
put anything past her."

"That's interesting. Very interesting." She'd bring Velma up
with Sergeant Hines and gauge his reaction. Maybe they could
add one more suspect to the growing list. She'd learned from

her few years writing for newspapers that usually the truth was stranger than any fiction she could have dreamed up. Even if it involved an old lady who looked too weak to defend herself, let alone kill the girl she blamed for her dear reverend's downfall.

Kelsey pulled out a business card from her front pocket and laid it on the counter. "It's been so nice talking to you. Let me know if you remember anything else."

Reverend Holiday glanced up when a knock sounded at his office door. Unable to sleep more than a few hours, he'd driven to the church early that morning, hoping to find peace among the familiar books and objects. It helped in times like this. No matter what else happened in the world, this was his sanctuary, this was his home.

He'd been at it for many hours now, while the day blazed outside. He tossed down his pen and rose. "Yes?"

The door swung open and a man in a starched white shirt and khakis entered. It was Harris Zeff, one of the church's long-standing deacons. Harris, a dignified man with salt-and-pepper hair and a kindly smile, sold life insurance during the week, while Saturdays he'd normally spend at his ranch tending to a few longhorns and alpacas he kept there. What was Harris doing in his office? And dressed in his business clothes, no less.

Harris didn't answer him. Didn't even acknowledge his question. When he silently stepped forward, he exposed another man behind him. Then another. A row of men filed into the reverend's office without saying a word. They all wore the same serious expression, as if they were pallbearers at a funeral.

Reverend Holiday counted the grim faces staring at him. Twelve men. The entire Board of Deacons had trickled into his office, some so reluctantly their backs grazed the wall. Many clasped their hands nervously in front of their bodies or studied their shoes. He glanced up and down the line. Was this about

Becca? Did the whole board know about him and the girl? The girl who had been found lying in a bayou by the Enterprise Police Department?

But they'd been so careful. They'd managed to keep their secret for months. Or so he thought. "Harris," he said. "Deacons' meeting was last night."

Harris cleared his throat and nodded vaguely at the men now lined up against the wall. "We know that."

"So then, what's all this about?" He took in the dozen men in their golf shirts and shorts, one or two wearing coveralls. Old Sam Derkins had managed to throw a blazer over his overalls, but he was sweating profusely. Served him right—all of them right—for ganging up on him like this.

"Maybe you'd better sit down, Reverend."

He wasn't about to let them tower over him. "If you don't mind, I'd rather stand."

Harris ignored the comment as if having the pastor in the same room was a formality. "We've come to a decision." Harris had come to say something and he was going to say it, no matter what. "And we've been praying." The deacon pointed again at the line to his right. Just above their shoulders hung an oil painting of Jesus and the disciples breaking bread at the Last Supper. How ironic. Was this a betrayal? Was Harris playing the role of Judas, about to expose him with a benign gesture?

"That's good, Harris. That's real good. I'm glad you're taking your duties seriously." A sea of blank faces stared at him. They had come to a decision about something, and it was an ominous decision.

"No one is accusing you of anything, Pastor. Let's make that perfectly clear. We don't want to believe you had anything to do with Miss Cooper going missing." He jerked his head back and forth, but his eyes looked doubtful. "That's a matter for the police."

Buddy Dent broke ranks with the others and stepped up close to the desk. He had a boyish face, but his features were rigid. "There's been a lot of talk." Buddy was young enough to be his son. "None of it good. We checked our Bibles and checked them again. It says clear as day that if a man can't control his household, he can't control a church."

My God. This was about Becca after all. They didn't believe him. They thought he had something to do with her death. It was as if Buddy had balled up his fist and jammed it into the reverend's diaphragm.

Harris spoke fast. "We didn't make this decision to hurt you."

Decision. So final. Everything seemed to slow down. Reverend Holiday lowered his gaze to the safety of the familiar desktop. "Gentlemen." He struggled to quell the quiver in his voice. "You caught me right in the middle of a sermon." He motioned at the papers scattered on the desk, but Harris was not about to give up.

"We'd like you to step down, Reverend. Before this scandal affects our church."

Our church. Reverend Holiday reeled. "Our church? Without me there isn't a church!"

"That's not true, Bobby."

He searched in vain for a sign. Some sign that this was all a big mistake. But not one of the men would return his gaze. The cowards. "You can't be serious."

They were obviously dead serious. Come to think of it, he'd been right about them preparing for a funeral. Only it was his funeral they were all there for.

"We want you to step aside," Harris repeated. "Or—"

"Or what? You're going to fire me after thirty years with this church?"

"Everyone knows you and Becca were together," Harris said. "Now that she's gone, there's going to be a lot of gossip. It'll only hurt the church. You don't want to hurt the church, now do you?"

He glared at Harris. Wanted to strike out, right then and there. How dare the deacon speak to him like that! Question his authority. How dare . . .

He collapsed into the chair, drained beyond measure. The deacon's words reverberated in his very soul, and he began to understand. They were right. That was the worst of it. They were right. There was nothing to be gained by him staying in the pulpit. The whispers and stares would drown out everything else, would shout down any sermon, any hope he had of being useful. They were all right. How often had he lectured these men standing around him now, towering above him? Lectured them to take their Bibles seriously. To study the words and apply them to their lives. Maybe he had taught them too well. Looks like he had taught himself right out of the pulpit.

A tear rolled down his cheek. "They found her body, Harris. Yesterday morning, over in the bayou. Oh, that precious little baby." He caught himself, too emotional to continue.

The twelve deacons stared at him, while behind their heads, the figure of Judas conspired to sell out his savior for a few pieces of silver.

No one spoke for the longest time. And when they did, it was only to say good-bye to the reverend, who softly wept in the confines of his armchair.

CHAPTER 7

After leaving Midway Liquors and returning to the newsroom—the jangle of bells preceding her—Kelsey logged onto her computer again, this time determined to finish her story.

Two of the strongest suspects in the death of Becca Cooper—Mr. and Mrs. Robert Holiday—both denied knowing about her death, let alone having anything to do with it. And, while she did have an excellent motive, LilliFay Holiday didn't look robust enough to take on a woman half her age. Neither did Velma Wainwright, for that matter.

Then, there was always the ex-husband in Oklahoma, who might or might not have been released by now. She knew Shawn Deschamps had found the body early Friday afternoon, and the girl had been dead for some time. She also knew Becca Cooper was four months' pregnant when she'd been killed, which seemed to upset Sergeant Hines more than anything else. There was still no murder weapon. Plus, the police sergeant in charge of the case had only a few days left until his retirement, even though he swore he'd find the culprit before then.

In all the months she'd been at the *Country Caller*—really only six or so, but it felt like forever—this was the most interesting story to come along. Before this, she'd been stuck writing about first-prize heifers and homecoming queens and the time some high school seniors dumped a load of laundry detergent into the courthouse fountain. Nothing like this had crossed her desk, ever. Even at her university, the most scandalous story she covered involved a professor plagiarizing a manuscript for a scientific journal. That was it. But, this was different. This was the kind of story her portfolio needed to bring it to life. To make an editor, somewhere, anywhere, sit up and take notice.

She began to type. Cautiously at first, then with more gusto as the theme emerged. While the police didn't have anyone in custody yet, they did have a condition of the body, at least two—if not three—"persons of interest," and a sergeant who wanted to end his career on a high note. Not a bad line-up for a front-page crime story.

And who knew? What if a local newswire service picked up on it? While the service didn't take important stories from little papers like hers—those were reserved for staff reporters—they did rely on places like the *Country Caller* for human interest stories, quick reads that might elicit a wince, or a chuckle. Things like oddball celebrations, reunions of long-lost family members, bungled holdups, maybe a small-town scandal . . . those were the stuff of wire stories. With one touch of a button, a wire service editor could send a small-town reporter's story zipping into the biggest newsrooms in the country. Kelsey might not get a byline, but she'd get a kick out of knowing her story had appeared in newspapers five states away. That somewhere in Louisiana, Mississippi, or even Florida, a reader would spot her story, never suspecting its author sat in a cramped newsroom next to a print shop in Enterprise, Texas.

Stranger things had happened. Maybe the editor would perk up when he heard the story's details. Maybe he'd—or she'd—deem it worthy to include in its line-up to member newspapers. That way the news would appear in the *Country Caller* first and Kelsey would get the credit, while other newspapers would get a juicy filler story. Everyone would win.

Of course, she felt awful for the murdered girl and her family, because no one deserved to die like that. Especially not a young girl in the prime of her life who was carrying someone's child. That's where Kelsey's work could help. As her favorite journalism professor back at the university liked to say, writing about crime was like shining a beacon into the shadows and chasing away the dark.

She logged onto the wire service's website to find the closest location for a news bureau. Not bad . . . just down the interstate, in Houston. Surely, everyone from the *Houston Sentinel* to the newspaper in San Antonio would subscribe to the wire service, if only to give them access to a buffet of regional stories from which to pick and choose. It'd be like handing her story directly to the news editor at a major paper. Since they paid for the service anyway, they might as well use it and get the latest local scandal instead of wasting their own reporter's time to cover it.

That's where Kelsey came in. She typed the story in a swirl of adrenaline.

Youth Makes Grisly Discovery on Bayou

May 12, Enterprise. The body of a missing church worker was discovered midday Friday on a bayou south of Enterprise. Police confirmed the identity of the victim as 28-year-old Becca Cooper, originally of Broken Arrow, Oklahoma.

Cooper, musical accompanist at Second Coming Charismatic Church, was determined to have suffered blunt trauma to the left side of her skull. According to Enterprise Police Sergeant George Hines, Cooper also was roughly four months pregnant.

"Until we receive the coroner's report, we can't speculate on the condition of the victim's body," said Sergeant Hines. "We've placed the time of death at approximately 8 A.M. Friday morning. Because this is an active investigation, we're asking the public to please contact us if they any have information to share."

According to Sergeant Hines, several area residents are being questioned as persons of interest. The name of the minor who discovered Cooper's body is not being released due to the youth's age.

According to county records, fewer than ten homicides have occurred in Enterprise over the past decade. Of those, four were determined to be self-defense and a fifth was dismissed for lack of evidence.

By the time Kelsey tore her eyes from the flickering screen, a half-hour had passed, then an hour, and now a hound dog slinked down Fifth Street, right in front of the *Caller*'s window, probably searching for an overturned dumpster. Sunshine swirled through a mosaic of dust on the plate glass. A mid-afternoon lull had settled over the town, and it seemed like she was the only person living in this corner of the world.

Her imagination began to swirl, as well. Yes . . . she would see about a job interview while the scandal was still hot. Convince an editor to check out her portfolio, give her a writing test. Maybe, someday soon, she could leave Enterprise behind.

Better yet, she might even get in good with a major Texas paper, work for a year or two, then angle for a job in Los Angeles. That was it. Swimming pools, movie stars.

She sighed, then forced herself to refocus on the desktop in front of her. Her story finished, she began to rifle through a pile of press releases that hulked on the desk's corner. She dug in and spent the next hour sorting through them, hoping to extract a workable story idea or two amid the rubble. She managed to pull a source for a possible feature, two news shorts. and a business "Q and A" from the bowels of the pile before coming up for air.

Finally, the rush of adrenaline that had propelled her through yet another hour of work began to wane. The tension knotting her shoulders gradually relaxed, as her fingers slid from the keyboard. She'd been up since dawn that morning . . . first to visit the police station, then Midway Liquors, then back here again.

It was all worth it, though. Now that her job was done, her shoulders relaxed, though her stomach ached from a lack of food.

She pushed her chair away from the desk. What would it be tonight? Barbecue . . . Chinese . . . Mexican? Though "Hog Heaven" lived up to its name, it would mean driving out of her way, so barbecue was out. And, the only Chinese restaurant in town never could get its noodles hot enough. Thankfully, the Grande Burrito always pleased. Plus, it was within shouting distance. So Mexican food would have to do.

She rose, and flicked off the overhead lights as she left the newsroom. After locking the door, she dragged herself a few short steps to the restaurant on the corner. She could see Bernie, the owner of the Grande Burrito, through the front window, leaning over a cash register toward the back of the place with a wad of bills in his hand and a confused look on his face.

A banner in the restaurant's window touted its world-famous taquitos, but the ambience inside suggested more "aloha" than "Azteca." The window shades sported hula girls wearing leis, crude palm trees had been painted in each of the window's corners, and a fake hibiscus sprouted on each table. Bernie definitely did not believe the adage that less was more, and the décor exploded in a riot of magenta, banana yellow, and lime green. Color, and more color, filled the space, except for one rectangle at the bottom of the front plate-glass window. There, someone had taped a black and white poster—of all things—to the inside of the glass.

Kelsey leaned toward the window for a better look. It was a show poster for an upcoming concert. Seems a local rock band called the "Witch Doctors" would play next weekend at the Grande Burrito. Mixed drinks only $2.50, all night long, the poster bragged. Bring a friend!

She studied a photo in the center of the poster. Five teenaged boys, all with jet-black hair and vacant stares, looked back at her. The kid behind the drum set looked familiar, and when she looked again, she realized it was Shawn Deschamps, the kid who had made the x-rated magazine magically disappear from his father's view.

She straightened, swung open the door to the restaurant, and immediately smelled hot vegetable oil and pressed limes. Bernie stood behind the register, still counting out bills. With his white hair and full beard, he reminded her of Santa Claus, if only Santa Claus wore Hawaiian shirts and flip-flops.

"Kelsey!" Bernie dropped the cash into the drawer and walked toward her, then enveloped her in a bear hug. "*Hola.* Table for one?"

"As usual. Just me, myself, and I." She followed him to a table at the side, empty save for a beer bottle filled with rock salt. Bernie opened his arms wide as she sat down.

"Mi casa es du casa."

"It's 'su' casa, Bernie." She spoke in a stage whisper. "You really should memorize that one if you're going to run a Mexican restaurant."

"Good thing I cook better than I talk." He jerked his head back to indicate the far wall of the restaurant. A ladder of glass shelves stair-stepped up to the ceiling, starting with the linoleum floor tiles and ending with acoustic ceiling squares. Shiny bottles of whiskey, gin, and mixes stood at attention. She knew the Grande Burrito made most of its sales from alcohol, usually during its concerts on the weekends.

"Hey, I saw the poster out front."

Bernie reached for a clean dishrag tucked into his apron. "Hold that thought." He ambled to the back, lifted a green bottle from the shelf, and returned. In quick succession he whisked two shot glasses from the same apron pocket and twisted off the cap on the gin. Clear liquid soon filled both of their shot glasses. "To Saturday nights!" He downed his drink in a single gulp.

She took a tiny sip from the glass. "I was saying . . . about the poster out front. Do you know those kids?"

Bernie wiped his hand across his moustache. "Course. They're from the high school."

"What do you know about Shawn?" Delicately, she set her glass down. "I heard he's a real troublemaker."

"Nah. He's a good kid. Misunderstood, but a good kid. You want an enchilada?"

"You got it. But about that kid. I went to see him today."

"Really?" Bernie pulled out an empty chair at the table and sat down. "Now, why would you go visit Shawn? Not that he's hard to find. Everyone knows where his dad's place is."

"That's the thing. I don't get it. Shawn and his dad are nothing alike. Is he adopted?"

Bernie poured another shot into his glass, but let it sit there while he spoke. "Nah . . . they're just night and day. His dad was a big deal in high school. Quarterback, I think. Guess it's hard for a kid like Shawn to live up to that, you know?"

Kelsey took another delicate sip from her glass. "I guess. So, you don't think he's trouble? Sergeant Hines said he's a bad seed. He's the one who found Becca Cooper's body."

Bernie flinched. "I didn't know that. I better give him a call. He might want to talk about it."

"So, you don't think . . ." She stopped right away when she saw a strange look cross Bernie's face.

"People always give that kid a hard time. They can't get past his hair, you know?" Anger flashed in Bernie's eyes. "If we had more kids like Shawn, there'd be a lot less trouble in the world. There's no way Shawn was involved. I would know . . . he tells me everything."

Clearly, she'd touched a nerve. But, why? She watched as Bernie rose, pushed the chair back toward the table, and left. So many loyalties in this town surprised her. Even if she lived a hundred years, she wasn't sure she'd be able to untangle them all. That's what made this story—this case—so complicated. She gulped her drink and waited for Bernie to return—hopefully with an enchilada.

CHAPTER 8

Come the next morning, LilliFay Holiday scurried into the sanctuary at Second Coming Charismatic Church, hoping to evade the prying eyes and curious glances of the people who had congregated for the nine-thirty service. When Bobby told her he planned to step down from the pulpit that morning, she didn't want to believe him. Couldn't believe him, not after all they'd been through.

Why, she'd stood by that man through everything: weddings, funerals, more Sunday night spaghetti suppers than she cared to count. She'd never resented it—she loved it, actually. Loved the feeling of being the woman of the house. Only, her house was a two-story cathedral with stained glass windows and a beautiful concert piano.

Which sat empty now. What with Becca Cooper gone, the choir director had no choice but to rely on the organist for the morning's hymns, with no accompaniment from the gleaming ebony piano. It was a shame, really. If he'd thought about it long enough or hard enough, surely he could have recruited one of the Sunday School teachers or maybe a member of his own chorus to play the piano for them that morning.

No matter. Having to sit through only half the music was the least of her worries. She scurried to the front of the church and slid into the first pew, like always. She was not about to hide in the back of the church, though that was what everyone no doubt expected her to do. How had things come to this? How had everything gone wrong so quickly?

She pretended to open her Bible and read from the first chapter. Already, she could feel eyes boring into the back of her head, right through the lavender hat she'd carefully picked out for the occasion. It was one of her favorites, and it gave her great comfort now, as she sat all by herself in the front row. Its extra-wide brim would provide enough protection to ward off the evil glances that would surely come her way.

She glanced over to the side of the sanctuary, to where Harris Zeff and a few of the other deacons sat. Such a comfort to know the church would go on, even without Bobby. Course the deacons were the ones who decided Bobby needed to step down, but she couldn't blame them, not really. She'd read that passage in Timothy about the leaders in the church and how they had to be responsible for their own homes. She knew that chapter by heart; she had read it so many times waiting up for Bobby on Thursday nights, knowing full well what he was up to but being unable to stop any of it.

Such a shame. Things could have ended so differently. Course, there was no telling where they might go now. Congregations the size of Bobby's didn't just grow on trees; she knew that. But still . . . they were in the Bible Belt, and odds were good that some church, somewhere, would need a pastor with Bobby's talent to run it. Maybe a struggling congregation in southwest Texas that knew nothing about the scandal back at Second Coming Charismatic Church. That didn't know about Becca Cooper and couldn't care less about her once they heard Bobby speak.

Maybe this was just the beginning. Maybe she and Bobby could start over now, like when they were first married. She glanced away from the row of deacons and focused on the pulpit, so impressive in the middle of the church. When Bobby rode into her hometown so many years ago, a traveling preacher back then on leave from a big church near Houston, she'd watched from the last row in the revival tent, mesmerized. Right then and there, she knew she was going to marry that man and make his life's work her life's work. It was the Lord's will. She knew that, watching him shout to the heavens, watching him move that revival audience to its feet like it had never been moved before.

When he up and proposed, it was the happiest day of her life. Finally, she had a cause that was big enough to believe in. Finally, she would make her Momma and Daddy proud and prove to everyone she was meant for bigger and better things. Who would have thought she'd be sitting here now, fanning herself with a bulletin, even though the air conditioner had been set to freezing for some unknown reason.

At long last, Bobby took to the pulpit. He gazed at the audience before him and actually smiled. Her heart fluttered at that. What a warrior. So what if he had defied the Lord's will and had gotten involved with Becca. Anyone could make a mistake, right? Anyone could sin. It was probably all Becca's fault, anyway. Her and that golden hair, that brilliant smile. What man could resist the charms of a woman a good twenty years younger than he was? It was no contest, and Becca must have known that all along.

The deacons rose from their seats now and formed a ring around Bobby. They wrapped their arms around him to form a tight circle and prayed over him, huddled like one of those football teams she saw on the sports channel sometimes. A huddle of black-suited men. It was enough to take her breath away. And then, just as she was watching the spectacle in front of her, she heard a voice, plain as day. A woman's voice. Calling to her. Speaking her name.

"Yes?" she answered. The deacons stopped their praying, and in a group, turned to look at her. Why, she hadn't done anything wrong. She was only answering that lovely, soft voice. LilliFay giggled and placed her finger against her lips, signaling she had no intention of speaking again.

The men returned to their mission of building a circle around her Bobby and invoking the Lord's name. Once again, a female voice floated down from the rafters, clear as day. A soft, musical voice, which rose and fell like a beautiful piano scale being played. It was too much for LilliFay. She couldn't resist the call of the voice, it being so lovely and all.

"Becca. Is that you?" LilliFay rose up to greet the voice. It would be rude to just sit there, now wouldn't it? She might be the wife of a disgraced preacher, but no one could ever accuse her of being rude. "I hear you, dear."

Someone in the audience gasped. LilliFay turned on her heel to face the congregation, all eight hundred and something of them. As usual, the place was packed to the rafters. The whole town had come to support Bobby, or condemn him. It was easy to see who fell into which camp. Bobby's friends sat near the front, clinging to the deacons' every move, while his detractors filled the balcony, like blood-thirsty Romans at the Coliseum. Surely they all heard Becca's voice?

"Are you angry, Becca? Is that why you've come?" She began to tremble now, the gravity of the situation sinking in. That Becca would rise up like this, just like Lazarus, was unthinkable. Surely the scandal was all behind them. Surely she wouldn't make any trouble now. "Don't hurt me, Becca. Please, don't hurt me." LilliFay's voice came out in a squeak, hardly her own voice at all.

The next thing she knew, two black-suited men descended on her and enveloped her in a bear hug. A comforting, warm bear hug. They would protect her. They would make Becca go away.

"Calm down," Harris told her. "We'll leave now, nice and quiet-like."

But she didn't want to leave. She wanted to stand by Bobby now that he really needed her. That was her job. She was a pastor's wife, after all.

"Ouch, Harris. You're pinching me." The deacon had wrapped his arm around her shoulders, but his grip was too tight. He obviously didn't know his own strength. The comforting bear hug felt smothering. She couldn't do anything but lean into the deacon and relent. Wherever he wanted to take her, she would calmly go. Anything was better than sitting in the front row of the church, watching Bobby hang his head in shame, watching him not even acknowledge her presence or what she had just gone through hearing the dead woman's voice. Anything was better than that.

"It's okay, Harris," she insisted. "I'll go with you. Just please don't squeeze so hard."

Harris didn't listen. He tried to hustle her out of the pew, like she was a common criminal. Like she was the one with the problem. Everything turned dark for LilliFay then, as she slumped against the deacon.

Kelsey watched the commotion from the balcony, amazed. Lilli-Fay Holiday had collapsed into the arms of one of the deacons, who half-carried, half-dragged her from the sanctuary with the help of another man.

Amazing. First off, she'd been surprised to even see LilliFay at church. When she'd visited Sergeant Hines yesterday, before she went to the newsroom, he tipped her off that the church had a big announcement to make the next day. So, come the next morning, she dragged herself out of bed, took a quick shower, and rushed over to Second Coming for the nine-thirty service.

Now, everything around her stilled, as the congregation watched the unfolding scene. Reverend Holiday stood frozen behind the pulpit, his head hanging. Clearly, it was anybody's guess what would happen next. Her eyes flitted from LilliFay as she left through a side door, to the mortified pastor, to the remaining deacons, who sat as inert as the stained glass figures behind them.

Finally the pastor seemed to recover, because he lifted his head and began to speak.

"Thank you for coming today. I'm sorry you had to witness that . . . so very sorry. This is a difficult day for all of us."

Kelsey scooted close to the edge of the pew, peering over the head of a stranger in front of her. Reverend Holiday looked exhausted, even from so far away. His handsome features sagged now. How could he stand there in front of a group of people who'd just witnessed the meltdown of his wife? Shouldn't he be out in the hall right now, attending to LilliFay?

"Some of you may have heard that Becca Cooper left us this week." The stranger in front of her coughed, but it sounded forced. That was an interesting way to put it. The reverend continued, "The Enterprise Police Department found her body . . . two days ago."

Gasps floated on the air. Reverend Holiday must have sensed their panic, because he spread his arms out dramatically. "We have to be strong as a church," he commanded them. "We can't let the devil take this opportunity to tear us apart."

A grandmother sitting next to Kelsey began to fan her face with a furious motion. Either people couldn't believe the news or they didn't want to, because most of them mutely watched the pastor speak.

"That's enough for one day," Reverend Holiday said, addressing the men who sat to the side of the stage. One by one the men nodded in approval. The big announcement must have been the recovery of Becca Cooper's body, which she already knew about. Oh, and apparently that the pastor's wife now spoke to dead people. She couldn't imagine she'd see much of LilliFay around town after that outburst. She guessed LilliFay would be "involuntarily committed" by the time the sun set, safely tucked out of sight until people's memories could wear thin around the edges.

The service ended, she rose and joined a stream of bodies that flowed from the balcony to the first floor. Reverend Holiday's news had affected the crowd in many ways. Some people looked bug-eyed, as if he'd just announced an alien invasion in the middle of Enterprise, while others looked doubtful, as if they must have heard wrong. A child skipped along nonchalantly, as if something like this happened every Sunday and she thought the grown-ups around her were weird anyway.

Kelsey arrived at the lobby in no time at all, and headed for an exit. Before she reached it, though, she spotted Velma, huddled with another woman by an alcove in the lobby. Sunshine poured through an open window above them. Whatever they were discussing, their heads bent together, Velma did not look pleased.

Kelsey ducked through the exit, then doubled outside to where the window had been flung open. She crushed a small daisy with her heel as she leaned close to the wall.

"Don't that just beat all!" Velma hissed. "That woman is still causing us trouble."

Funny, she would have thought Velma would be concerned for LilliFay, or at least feel sorry for her. She didn't expect her to complain about the pastor's wife so openly. When her shoe began to sink into the flower bed, Kelsey stepped onto a garden stone and balanced between the mushy soil and hard rock.

"How dare she cause all of this commotion," Velma continued. "No telling what people are thinkin' now . . . there's just no telling."

Kelsey leaned close to the window, favoring the foot set on the mossy stone.

"I'll say this . . . I'm glad she's gone. There. I said it. Most people would think that a sin, but I don't care."

Kelsey had no idea Velma felt that way about LilliFay Holiday. How many hurts must have built up for her to speak out like that? So much bad blood must have passed between the two women for Velma to throw caution to the wind and unload like this. LilliFay's outburst in church must have struck Velma to the core.

"Yes, sir." Velma said. "I'm glad Becca Cooper's not here anymore to torture the Holidays. When I think of all the hurt that woman's caused, I could just scream."

Kelsey pulled back from the window. Velma's rant wasn't directed at LilliFay. It was Becca Cooper she hated.

"Now maybe we can find some peace around here." Velma's voice fell silent then, lost in the revving of car engines and the chatter of a dispersing crowd. Maybe the liquor store owner— Deschamps—was right about Velma, after all. If she harbored such hatred for Becca Cooper, maybe she was capable of much more.

Kelsey stepped away from the window. At this point, everyone was suspect in the young woman's murder. Even a five-foot-tall secretary who clearly idolized her boss and hated his young mistress.

Kelsey returned to the path to join the throng of people streaming out of the church. Now she felt more confused than ever.

CHAPTER 9

As usual, Kelsey was the first to arrive in the newsroom come Monday morning. Renee wouldn't be in until nine o'clock or so, which meant a whole hour of peace and quiet. Even the guys running the printing press next door usually took a break at eight to grab a cup of coffee and a smoke before firing the machine up again.

She loved this time of day. No phones ringing, no one yelling at her to file her story *or else,* no interruptions of any kind. A chance to log onto Houston's biggest newspaper and read about the comings and goings of the country's fourth largest city. Or, if she was feeling particularly wistful, she could log onto the website for the paper in L.A. and dream she was sitting at a computer there, writing about corruption scandals or raging wildfires, not describing the line-up for this year's Mayfest in Heritage Park.

Of course, now that a scandal brewed at Second Coming Charismatic Church, things were starting to heat up in Enterprise, too. Maybe it could give the big cities a run for their money, or at least give her something interesting to write about for the first time in forever.

She flicked her computer on and began to type in her password. The tinny sound of the sleigh bell interrupted her, and a figure entered the room, visible over the top of her computer screen, wearing a crisp white shirt and khakis. The man looked a little like the deacon from church yesterday, the one who had whisked LilliFay Holiday from the building after she had made a scene. Funny . . . from the balcony he'd looked a lot shorter.

"May I help you?"

"Morning," he said with a nod. "I'm looking for the man who wrote a story Saturday." He glanced around the newsroom before continuing. "Fellow by the name of Kelsey Garrett."

She grinned. Used to bother her no end when people would assume her name meant she was a boy, but that was before high school, when she realized gender-neutral names had their own advantages. Like throwing off substitute teachers and intimidating visitors when they read the starting line-up for the girls' basketball team. "That's me," she said proudly.

"I'm sorry, miss. I just assumed—"

"Don't be." Come to think of it, she was a little surprised by his reaction. After what the liquor store owner had told her—not to mention Park Daniels—she thought everyone had been given a bio about her when she first came to town. No matter. "What can I do for you?"

The stranger stepped forward. "Name's Harris Zeff." He approached her desk and briskly shook her hand.

"I know who you are," she said. "You're a deacon at the church. I saw you yesterday, helping out with the pastor's wife."

He withdrew his hand. "Well, I'm sorry you had to see that. We don't normally air our dirty laundry."

Kelsey motioned to an oak chair sitting in front of her desk. The stranger accepted it and eased in his lanky frame. Silver haired, with smooth, tanned skin, he reminded her of an old-time Hollywood cowboy. All that was missing was the six-shooter and a horse.

"It was quite a show," Kelsey said. "What do you think set off LilliFay like that?" She knew darned well, after speaking with Sergeant Hines and LilliFay, but it'd be interesting to hear how this man framed it.

Harris glanced around the newsroom before speaking. "How much do you know about our church?"

"Well . . . I know you're popular. Looks like the whole town was there yesterday."

"That's true," he agreed. "That's what's made this whole affair so painful. I don't know if anyone's told you this, Miss Garrett, but our pastor and Miss Cooper were more than friends, if you catch my drift."

Kelsey cocked her head. "Why are you telling me this, Mr. Zeff?" It wasn't every day that people sought out a reporter to spill out what they thought was a shocking secret.

"Well, some strange things have been going on around the church." He clasped his hands together and looked at her intently. "It's not like us to have a crime wave in Enterprise."

"Crime wave? Miss Cooper's death is a terrible tragedy, but I wouldn't exactly call it a crime wave. Would you?"

"Oh, but there's more." He began to rub his hands together studiously. "This past week alone something very important was taken from our church."

"Really?" Kelsey regretted not firing up her computer earlier. But, then again, taking notes while someone was talking to her was a surefire way to get them to shut up. Most people hated having their words committed to paper, she'd found. More often than not, she liked to scribble a few notes in the margins of her reporter's notebook, rather than distract the speaker by glancing down at a page every other second.

"It's strange, that's all I can say about it. Every week now, for twenty years, right before I leave the deacons' meeting on Friday night, I set out the elements for the Lord's Supper." He illustrated by pretending to place a cup on her desk, next to the computer. "Put the plate and the chalice right there in their places so no one has to go looking for them. Except for two nights ago." He looked at her in wonder. "When I go to get the chalice from its case, and it's gone. It's plumb not there." He studied his empty hands, as if amazed by the void. "Now, I had to ask myself, who would steal something like that?"

"Have you told Sergeant Hines?" Much as she wanted to help this man, who'd entrusted her with his deep concern, she didn't know what use she could be. "You'll have to fill out a stolen property report."

"Yes, I understand." He snapped out of his reverie and nodded toward her computer screen. "But after reading your story Saturday, I thought you might find it interesting. Nothing like this has happened in Enterprise before, and you just have to ask yourself why. Sometimes, don't you ask yourself why?"

She smiled for the second time that morning. "Every day, Mr. Zeff. It's my job. What you're telling me is you think the burglary is tied to Miss Cooper's murder. Is that what you're saying?"

"I don't see how it couldn't be, Miss Garrett. It's just too coincidental." He leaned forward. "You see, I've been selling insurance for a long time. We cover everything . . . fire, theft, floods. All kinds of things no one plans for. But this seems planned to me. Two strikes against one church, after all these years." He nodded his head for emphasis. "Yes, I think the murder and the theft had something to do with each other."

She heard the tinny sleigh bell ring again, and glimpsed Renee as she walked through the front door of the newsroom.

"Keep that in mind, Miss Garrett, when you're writing your stories," the deacon told her as he rose. "Someone is waging war against the church."

A crescendoing hum of cicadas filled the morning air on Monday as Bobby walked out the front door to retrieve his morning newspaper. Dressed in a gray suit and blood-red tie, humidity immediately enveloped him like a thick, wet blanket.

Strange how the rest of the world seemed unchanged. He could hear the whine of a school bus in the distance, making one of its last runs of the year. A pet chicken clucked in the yard of the retired farmer two doors down. Even the cicadas seemed uninterested in him, as they serenaded each other with their singing.

While outwardly nothing seemed different, everything had changed. The deacons didn't give him a timeline, but he assumed they wanted him to step down as soon as possible. Sweep the whole thing under the rug. Crazy to think that after all these years, his life as a minister would come down to this.

He scooped up the newspaper and retreated to the house. Once safely inside, he heard the sound of water beating against shower tile. He and LilliFay rarely saw each other in the morning, because usually he was up and out of the house well before sunrise, and he assumed she slept until mid-morning or so. He shuffled into the kitchen and laid the plastic-sheathed newspaper on the counter.

Breakfast. How long had it been since he'd had breakfast in his own home? The folks at the fast-food place would wonder when they didn't see his sedan in the drive-through line. One black coffee and two egg sandwiches usually held him until lunchtime, when he would close his office door and tear into the sack lunch LilliFay would have prepared for him. Then he'd find meatloaf or homemade potato salad or sweet pumpkin pie wrapped in wax paper. Now, when he opened the refrigerator, an empty spot greeted him on the top shelf where his lunch should have been.

Such was the life of a man of God. He grabbed for some eggs in the holder and shut the refrigerator door. After fumbling around in the drawer for a suitable pan, he withdrew a skillet and set it on the burner. No need to impress someone in his own home, so he shrugged off the suit jacket and draped it over one of the kitchen chairs. Hearts and flowers scrolled across the pine chair's back. So fussy, but LilliFay seemed to like it.

"Here, let me do that." LilliFay appeared in the doorway in a terrycloth bathrobe, her hair done up in a turban. Truth be told, she was a handsome woman with strong features and eyes that still sparkled, after all these years.

He nodded gratefully. He didn't know what to do with the eggs anyway. Somehow, he'd hoped a recipe would come to him when he started. Instead, he reached for a coffee cup LilliFay had placed on the counter, a delicate cup wild with roses.

"You're up early," she said as she gathered the eggs.

"Same for you," he countered. As coffee slowly trickled into his cup, he inhaled the earthy scent. Coffee from the drive-through line never smelled this good.

"Why are you all dressed up?" She cracked an egg on the lip of the skillet.

"Thought I'd go into work today. See what's going on." In all honesty, he didn't know what else to do. The routine was part of him now. He could no more have stopped dressing and leaving for work than that chicken could have stopped its scratching in the farmer's back yard a few doors down.

"Do you think that's smart?" LilliFay didn't turn to face him. She continued to break one egg after another into the frying pan.

"I have to face this, LilliFay. Nothing's going to bring Becca Cooper back, but I can't sit here in this house and pretend nothing's happened. People want answers. And, if they don't get them from me, they're going to start making up their own."

Slowly, LilliFay began to stir the egg whites with a spatula. He didn't have to ask her to separate the yolks; she did it automatically. She knew how he liked them. "Do you know who killed her, Bobby?"

He puffed out his cheeks before speaking. "That's a fine question to ask your own husband." He'd already spent hours running through conversations like this in his mind. What did he know, and when did he know it? People would have a million questions for him, but he didn't expect LilliFay to be one of them. "Don't you think I would've told the police if I did?"

"I guess so." Finally, she turned to face him after laying the spatula on the edge of the range. "Have a seat and I'll bring these to you."

The kitchen seemed so small now, really too small for both of them. "I've got to wash up." He left LilliFay standing beside the range with one sleeve of her robe rolled to the elbow, and started down the hall. The powder room—as LilliFay liked to call it—was just off the foyer.

While he never used the room himself, he knew LilliFay kept it stocked with lavender soap and fancy blue guest towels, which he wouldn't find at the kitchen sink. Come to think of it, he felt like a guest now as he walked through the living room of his own house. Maybe it was the way sunlight splashed across the worn sofa, or striated the powder-blue rug. LilliFay always did have a fancy for blue. And angels. Dozens of them, lining the walls, running from crown molding to baseboards. Big ones, little ones, all of them painted gold. Here and there a cherub would dance among the faces, its fat body discreetly covered by a ruffled scroll. How she had found so many cherubs in different shapes and sizes was beyond him.

He reached the end of the wall, the intersection of the living room and foyer. Down low, a bare spot caught his eye. Judging by the perfect outline pressed into the flowered wallpaper, one of the cherubs was missing. Not only that, but it had been a large one that took up twice the space of the others.

"LilliFay," he called to her from the hall. "Whatever happened to the cherub that goes here?" He looked up to see her lean away from the stove.

"Goes where? What are you talking about?"

He pointed to the blank spot on the wall, though he guessed she would have no idea what he was pointing at. Couldn't really, not from her place in the kitchen. "There's one missing. From the wall. Right here."

"Honestly, Bobby. I'm going to burn your eggs. What are you talking about?"

"Didn't you have something here, on the wall?" Judging by the ring it left, whatever had been placed against the wall had been there for a long time.

"I don't think so. Go wash up now. You don't want your breakfast to cool."

"No, I'm sure of it. There used to be something right here. One of the big ones. Right?"

"Keep this up and your eggs are going to be ruined," she warned him.

No, he distinctly remembered seeing a figurine there. Had grazed it once, with his calf. Oversized, it had reminded him of one of the fat babies Michelangelo might have painted. It wasn't like LilliFay to let something go like that. Not with her being so fastidious with the rest of the house. He wandered out of the hallway, and into the kitchen. His hands weren't that dirty anyway, and LilliFay sounded annoyed. Best not to start this day off by arguing with her. Heaven only knew that there were enough arguments waiting for him back at the church.

Kelsey scooped the newspaper from the lawn with one hand as she shielded her eyes with the other. The cicadas were out in full force this Tuesday morning, running up and down their scales from a patch of bushes in front of her rented cottage.

The first time she saw the place, she fell in love. The realtor had warned her about the cottage's low ceilings and leaky windows, but she wouldn't listen. She loved the pitched roof and wooden shingles, shutters that bookended every window, a tire swing hanging from a sturdy oak out front. If the Brothers Grimm had lived in Enterprise, Texas, they surely would have set one of their stories here.

She straightened—newspaper in hand—and hopped back onto the brick path. Fortunately, the cement still felt cool, given that she had nothing on but a pair of boxer shorts and an old t-shirt. No need to dress up when there was lots of land between the houses. Which her realtor thought was a problem, but which she loved. After bouncing around from one college apartment to another, where there were never enough bathrooms or paper towels or privacy, the idea of living among a stand of pin oaks appealed to her. Nothing like waking up first thing in the morning and tromping around in the altogether if you damned well felt like it.

She stepped through the doorway and shut the heavy panel behind her. The newspaper glistened, and she pulled the plastic tight to peek at the headline before anything else. There, for all the world to see, ran twelve-point type with her byline directly underneath. Her name wavered behind the film, but a chill pinballed down her spine, as always. What a rush. Forget the fancy salaries and the expensive cars. She'd take her name in Times New Roman font any day of the week.

She practically skipped to the kitchen. Painted bright yellow, with a line of dancing cherries sprinkled across the ceramic backsplash, it'd become her favorite room in the house. Even though she didn't cook—adding milk to Kraft macaroni and cheese was about as far as she got in that department—she loved to hunch over the kitchen table with a copy of the newspaper in one hand and a mug of coffee in the other. Those days the newspaper didn't print out, she'd have to read the back of a cereal box.

She peeled back the plastic and laid the newspaper flat on the kitchen table. There was her article, all right, front and center. With a picture of Sergeant George Hines splat in the middle. From his quotes, now the whole town would know the murdered girl had been four months pregnant when she died. Other than a few "persons of interest," the police had yet to close in on a suspect.

Just then, a slim telephone hanging on the wall jangled, interrupting her thoughts. She leaned back and half-heartedly lifted the handset from the receiver.

"Good morning! Hope I didn't wake you."

Instantly, she recognized the voice. It was Park, the man she'd met at church Friday night. The one with the beautiful eyes and old-fashioned manners. The one in the picture with Becca Cooper, too. She straightened her shoulders. "Not at all. Good morning." She smiled, even though he couldn't see her.

"Got your number from someone in your office yesterday. Hope you don't mind."

"That's alarming. They're not supposed to give my phone number out. How'd you get them to give it to you?" She could imagine it'd have been a lot easier if Park had made a visit to the newsroom. Renee would be no more able to resist his good looks than she had been.

He chuckled into the telephone "Said I had a fix-it job going over at your house and I'd lost your number. Don't forget, we're a pretty tight community around here."

She swiveled around in the chair until she faced the table again. "Well, that's comforting. What else did they give you . . . my social security number?"

"I wish." He chuckled again. "Seriously, though, I thought I'd see you around town this weekend, but no luck."

"Oh . . . this weekend." She didn't have the heart to tell him she'd been out chasing leads in Becca Cooper's death all weekend. No need to come across as a workaholic quite so soon. "I must have been busy. Sorry about that."

"Hmmm. Bet you were working, weren't you?"

Was it that obvious? "You caught me. This whole murder thing has got me going around in circles."

The line fell silent. Immediately she regretted bringing up Becca Cooper's death. However, her eyes fell on the newspaper and a possible way out. "Have you read the newspaper yet? That's my story on the front page."

She heard Park whistle under his breath. "Honestly? That'll make you famous around here. Not as famous as the football team, but that's a whole 'nother story. But that's not why I'm calling."

She tucked a strand of hair behind her ear, hoping to bring his voice even closer.

"You still have to eat, right? I've heard that even reporters have to break down and eat once in a while."

"Once in a while," she agreed. She focused on steadying her voice, which had a tendency to rise when she got excited.

"Good. How about I take you out to dinner tonight? You know, to celebrate your big newspaper story and all. We might even need a bodyguard," he teased.

"Ha, ha. Despite your sarcasm, I accept the offer." Her voice had definitely risen a notch.

"Okay, then. I'll pick you up around six. That okay with you?"

She nodded her head, even though he couldn't see her from where he sat. "That'd be fine." She'd managed to control the pitch of her voice, but she still sounded like an eager teenager. She felt like she was throwing herself at a perfect stranger, albeit one with the most amazing eyes ever, so she forced herself to stay quiet.

"Tonight then," he said, before hanging up the phone.

"Tonight," she whispered to the receiver. Slowly, she hung

the telephone back on its handset. Not bad. A front-page story in the *Country Caller,* and a good-looking man asking her on a date. What else could possibly happen?

CHAPTER 10

It took Kelsey only five minutes or so to drive from her cottage to downtown Enterprise once she'd showered and dressed for the day. After hanging up the telephone with Park, she checked her refrigerator but found only a stick of butter and a shriveled lemon, so it was time, once again, to visit the Grande Burrito for some breakfast.

There was nothing grand about it, but Bernie made a mean breakfast burrito stuffed with eggs, white cheese, and home-grown tomatoes. She parked in front of the strip center and breezed through the plate-glass door, the only one in the place on this Tuesday morning.

Bernie was there, wearing his usual Hawaiian shirt and flip-flops. The restaurant was an anomaly in so many ways. Alongside the beef fajitas and chicken enchiladas, Bernie offered organic taco salads made with arugula and tofu. Instead of mariachi music, patrons heard Jimmy Buffet and the Beach Boys. Tired of margaritas? Guests were invited to bring their own liquor, provided they share some with the owner. The place was quirky, but she loved it.

Bernie had emerged from behind a serape that shielded the kitchen from the dining tables, which was probably a good thing.

"Morning, Kelsey." He greeted her with an affable grin. If Santa Claus had come to Enterprise—and he surfed—he'd look like Bernie, she thought once again. He'd told her once he only grew the silver beard to hide bits of nacho that dribbled onto his chin, and she believed him.

"A breakfast burrito, please. Don't skimp on the salsa this time."

"You got it. Sit anywhere you want. Tables are clean today."

"That's a miracle." She picked a table near the front, by a smudged window that overlooked Fifth Street. Butter sizzled on the grill as he set about making her burrito.

"How's business?" she yelled to the serape.

"Up and down, but mostly up. Must be my cooking."

"Don't flatter yourself. It's the ambiance." She brushed some salt crystals off the paper placemat. "Time to wipe down the tables again."

"Hired someone new to do that. Didn't I tell you?" His voice floated through the serape, accompanied by the crackle of hot grease.

"No, you didn't."

He emerged from the kitchen with her burrito and a cup of coffee. "This guy was looking for a job, so I thought I'd give him a chance."

She accepted the plate and mug. "Thank you. So, when's he start?"

"Already started. Want more salsa?" He waved his hand back, toward the kitchen. Nothing stirred behind the curtain though.

"I'm good." She dug into the breakfast, as Bernie talked up the band that was going to play at the restaurant Saturday night. He still couldn't get over Shawn Deschamps finding the body of Becca Cooper.

She finished her burrito and a cup of coffee, before wadding her napkin up next to her plate. "Excellent, as usual." This time, Bernie had let the cheese melt a little longer until it coated the burrito in a warm, thick glaze. "One of your best yet."

"Tell your friends and neighbors." He winked at her.

"How much do I owe you?" Usually, her breakfasts ran about

five bucks or so, but every once in a while she splurged and added organic mushrooms to the mix, which upped the ante.

"It's free today. Just for you."

Unfortunately, Bernie wasn't the best businessman in town. He was known for buying every fundraising cookie imaginable, then turning around and donating them to the city of Enterprise for the annual Mayfest picnic. Any time someone needed a handout, they knew where to come. She liked that about him, but it must have been hard on his business. "No, really. Add it to my tab."

"If you insist. But if you leave a tip, I'll brain you."

She rose to her feet, stuffed with egg whites and caffeine. "You're killing my diet, Bernie."

He scooped up her plate, and laid her knife and fork crosswise on it. "Saw your story today about the murder. You're gonna be famous if you don't watch out."

"Hopefully."

"Just be careful, okay?" Bernie's smile had disappeared. "Some people don't like it here when you tell the truth. You're shaking things up, and that makes 'em nervous."

"Do tell." She began to lumber toward the door. As she reached for the door's handle, a stranger brushed past her, obviously in a hurry. She stepped aside to let him through, and as she did, glimpsed the dirty blond hair and craggy cheeks she'd seen somewhere before. The man hurried past her and disappeared through the serape, headed for the kitchen.

It couldn't be, could it? The stranger's profile fit the mug shot she'd glimpsed on the Internet yesterday, the one that ran with the story of the husband who beat Becca Cooper so badly she ended up in the intensive care unit. Same straggly blond hair, same watery green eyes, same weathered cheeks and chin. But that would be impossible. Becca's husband lived in Oklahoma, for goodness sake.

"Hey, Bernie." She turned away from the door to face him. Bernie stood at the table, as he balanced her plate and silverware in one hand and coffee mug in his other. "That guy you hired to help out. Was he from Enterprise?"

The cutlery clanked against the plate as Bernie rearranged the load in his arms. In the background, she heard the sound of water filling a tub, or maybe it was the sink. That and the sound of someone whistling along to Jimmy Buffet's "Cheeseburger in Paradise." "Nah. He came here from Oklahoma. Said something about a fresh start."

Even though a hot summer sun blazed all around them and her body had been warmed by coffee, Kelsey shivered. Only once, but enough to stop her cold, right there in the middle of the Grande Burrito on Fifth Street.

Once she regained her wits, Kelsey said good-bye to Bernie and headed next door to the newsroom. The sleigh bell jangled as she flung the door open and walked in. She still couldn't believe how similar the stranger at Bernie's looked to the mug shot of Becca Cooper's former husband. *Impossible.* Wasn't it?

She flicked on the overheads and yanked open the mini-blinds to the large picture window that overlooked Fifth Street. Sunlight poured into the space, illuminating the gaps between the computers and printers, the file cabinets stuffed full of news-paper clippings, the manila file folders that held decades' worth of ad mock-ups and client invoices. Dust specks swirled prettily in the still air as if remnants from the night before, splintered by the bright sunshine.

She headed for her own desk and fired up her computer for the day. She'd decided over the coffee that today was the day she would send her story to the wire service in Houston and see where it led. She logged onto the *Caller*'s website and saw her story, bannered as the lead article for the week. Given the option to email the text to another address, she typed in the wire service's web address and watched the screen go blank as the story flew from her computer to theirs. She'd know in an hour or two if they were interested; that was the beauty of it. An hour equaled an eternity in newspaper time, so no more than two should pass before she'd have her answer. Time enough to call Sergeant Hines and see what was new in Becca Cooper's murder investigation.

She reached for the telephone, but the jangling of sleigh bells made her pause. For the second day in a row, an early morning visitor had come to the *Country Caller's* offices. Plus, the smell of flowers wafted in with the newcomer . . . lots of flowers. Mingling with the smell of dusty folders and printer's ink.

When she swiveled around, a woman was poised in front of her desk, framed by the picture window. It was LilliFay Holiday, dressed head to toe in lavender. What was more surprising? To see LilliFay Holiday out and about, when Kelsey thought they might admit her to the county hospital after Sunday's outburst, or to behold the shiny purple shirt, lavender pocketbook pressed close to the woman's chest, and the enormous purple hat? She blinked to confirm the sight. LilliFay looked much too bright for the small, harsh space.

"Hello, Miss Garrett." LilliFay glanced to the empty oak chair pushed against Kelsey's desk, as if waiting for an invitation to sit down. Kelsey mutely nodded and pointed to the empty chair.

"Don't mind if I do," LilliFay said with a flourish.

As LilliFay lowered herself into the chair, Kelsey spied a black book, its pages edged in gold, peeking from the top of her pocketbook. She'd been preached to once before by LilliFay, and she wasn't looking to repeat that experience. Better to ask her own questions before LilliFay had a chance to railroad the conversation. "Good morning, Mrs. Holiday. To what do I owe this pleasure?"

LilliFay smiled demurely. "Now don't be so formal. You know you can call me LilliFay. Everyone else does."

To be truthful, LilliFay looked more like a fluffy standard poodle than a flesh-and-blood woman sitting there, all powdered and painted and ready to show. "How can I help you?"

LilliFay giggled. "You're all business, that's for sure. I wanted to come by and talk to you about this story with Becca Cooper."

Of course. She probably wanted to let her have it now that Kelsey had all but named her as a suspect in the first story—the one about Becca Cooper's disappearance. She gritted her teeth in anticipation.

"We need to make sure you have the full story, honey." Lilli-Fay leaned forward and placed a purple-clad arm on the desk, releasing a second wave of perfume. "We don't want to write anything that's not true, do we?"

Kelsey cocked her head. "Of course." Now, why would the wife of the pastor of the town's largest church, a woman who had been half-led, half-dragged from that very church only a day ago, decide to pay Kelsey a visit in the newsroom?

"The way I see it," LilliFay said, "the Enterprise Police Department is going to need all the help it can get, if you catch my drift." She nodded earnestly, fully committed to whatever she'd come to say. "If you haven't noticed, they're a little short-staffed."

"I'd noticed." Which was the truth, but not unusual for a town the size of Enterprise. Most small towns made do with a sergeant, a deputy or two, and some volunteers on the side. Apparently, LilliFay didn't think much of the Enterprise Police Department, though, because she crinkled her nose.

"I'm not sayin' they don't know what they're doing. I'm just sayin' we need to help them whenever we can. Which is why I'm here today."

"Why *are* you here today, Mrs. Holiday?" Whatever it was that LilliFay had come to say, she seemed to be taking her sweet time about it. Not that Kelsey minded, because it beat having LilliFay berate her for naming names in the first story.

"We all know Miss Cooper wasn't exactly a saint, God bless her." LilliFay lowered her eyes respectfully. When she glanced up again, those eyes sparkled brightly. "She had a way with the men, if you know what I mean."

Kelsey toyed with the idea of typing down notes as LilliFay spoke, but didn't. Better to let the preacher's wife speak freely, unselfconsciously. "I'd heard."

"Who could blame them? With her looks and figure, I don't. Course, heaven only knows I've landed my fair share of men." LilliFay reached into her pocketbook and began to root around for something.

Please, not the Good Book. Don't start flipping through the Bible again and thumping the battered pages, she wanted to implore her. Luckily, LilliFay withdrew a newspaper clipping instead, so thin from use that light shone straight through it. Yellowed, bisected with a neat fold, she held it up for Kelsey's inspection.

It took Kelsey a moment to recognize the young faces beaming at her from the newspaper clipping. The man, barely old enough to shave, it seemed, looked like a younger version of Reverend Holiday, complete with shoe-polish black hair and shiny cheeks. Next to him stood LilliFay, her hair swept up like one of the girls from a fifties movie, the folds beneath her cheeks gone. A wedding portrait, it was.

"Don't we look amazing?" LilliFay asked, her voice tinged with awe. "That's me and Bobby on our wedding day." She gazed at the picture as if it'd appeared in the newspaper that morning, not decades earlier.

"Mmm-hmm," Kelsey agreed, for once lost for words. That LilliFay would cart around a newspaper clipping from thirty years earlier struck her as excessive, even for her.

"See, I had my day, too. Guess everybody does. I can't blame Becca Cooper for using what the good Lord gave her. Heaven only knows that Park Daniels isn't too bad to look at, either."

"Excuse me?" Kelsey glanced up from the photograph. "What does he have to do with this?"

"I'm just saying you need to have the full story about Becca Cooper if you're going to nose around this town for information." LilliFay finally tore her eyes away from the newspaper clipping, as well. "Park and Becca were quite the item for a while. Which I didn't mind, because it kept her away from my Bobby."

Calmly, LilliFay returned the newspaper clipping to her purse and clasped it shut. "Maybe you should be asking Park Daniels about Becca Cooper. That's all I'm saying. I'd hate for you to get only half the story." With that, LilliFay rose from the chair. "You don't know much about us, do you? The next time you speak with Sergeant Hines, mention Park's name to him. I'm sure he'll be mighty interested."

She stood over Kelsey's desk now and pointed to the computer, which hummed ever so softly. "Type that in your story, honey. We wouldn't want you to lead people astray."

Kelsey recovered just long enough to call out to LilliFay as the woman stepped toward the door. "I'm surprised to see you here today. After those men took you away, and all."

"Who . . . the deacons? They're harmless. I had to promise them I'd start taking my medication again, is all."

LilliFay's smile slipped when she stepped onto the sidewalk outside the *Country Caller Gazette*. Thank goodness that was over. She knew she could do it, if she just put her mind to it. She skipped a few steps down the walk, until she remembered the picture window and straightened properly for the benefit of the young reporter probably watching her from the other side.

She had every right to be mad at Kelsey Garrett, but this way was much better. Daddy always did say that it was easier to catch flies with honey than vinegar. So what if she had to bite her tongue? The whole thing had lasted only a minute or two, and if talking to that reporter helped her Bobby even a smidgen, it was worth it.

Bobby. She'd done this whole thing for him. Not that he deserved it, of course. What he deserved was for LilliFay to hightail it back into that newsroom and tell that young woman exactly what she knew. To confess that a few days back, the night Becca Cooper disappeared, her beloved Bobby hadn't returned home until almost sunup.

At first, she thought maybe he'd spent the night at the condo again, though she believed with all her heart that he'd finally given up this nonsense with Becca. When he didn't come home by midnight, she convinced herself that something at church must be keeping him late, and she'd hear his car in the drive any minute.

That's when she turned off the television set and trudged back to their bedroom, which looked as cold and empty as she felt. She'd come to dread Thursday nights, after Harris told her exactly where Bobby had been going those past few months. The next morning, after Harris told her that, she started her own tradition. She marched straight to the corner market and bought a copy of a racy magazine, which she tucked away in her nightstand until the following week. When Bobby left for the condo the next Thursday, she dredged up the issue and ogled the male models for a good hour, just to get back at him. The Bible said that if you lusted in your heart, it was about the same as lusting in the flesh, so she might as well enjoy her own sinful thoughts if Bobby couldn't even come home to his very own wife.

But that Thursday had been different. She could feel it in her bones when Bobby looked her straight in the eye and said he had something to attend to at church. She shouldn't have, but she believed him that time. He didn't glance away like he normally did, and he didn't grab his car keys with a trembling hand. He actually kissed her good-bye, which hadn't happened any other time. She knew he was going to the church that night.

So, come about midnight, when he still hadn't come home, she retreated to their bedroom, wondering what had made her think that things would be different. She dozed fitfully, each time thinking that if she rolled over, she'd see Bobby's sleeping form on the edge of their bed. One time, two times, three times. Finally, she dropped off for good and didn't wake up again until the neighbor's rooster crowed at sunrise.

This time, Bobby's slumbering figure rose and fell as he slept in his usual spot on the bed, fully clothed. She couldn't imagine what would have kept him away for so many hours and drained him to the point he'd collapsed onto the bed in his good clothes. Truth be told, she was too mad to care, since he'd promised he'd be home early. Since he'd raised her hopes like that, only to dash them to pieces. If it wasn't Becca at the condo, then what had kept him out all night?

Now, as LilliFay stood on the sidewalk just beyond the newsroom door, she exhaled loudly. That's what she should have told the young reporter. That's what Bobby deserved. He would never know what measures she took to protect him. No, he'd never know the lengths she went to.

Once LilliFay flounced out of the newsroom, taking the sickly sweet smell of lavender with her, Kelsey leaned back in her chair and stared at the flickering computer screen. She'd wondered why Park seemed so reticent to talk about Becca Cooper back at the sanctuary. Now she had her answer.

My, but Becca had been busy. So far, she knew that Bobby Holiday and now Park Daniels had both been smitten with her. A sour taste appeared in the back of Kelsey's throat, which was ridiculous, because Park had every right to date whomever he wanted to. His love life wasn't any of her business. Just because he and Becca had been an item before her death didn't mean anything . . .

Or did it? There was no way she could stay in the newsroom any longer and concentrate, what with the image of Park monopolizing her thoughts and causing everything else to recede into the background.

She scooped her purse from the floor and flung it over her shoulder. She still had some time before Renee would make it into work, more than enough time to pay a visit to Enterprise's finest. Sergeant Hines would know what to make of this connection, and if he didn't, she'd have to wait until her dinner date with Park to have her questions answered.

As she drove along Fifth Street, she struggled to collect her thoughts. There, on her right, stood Second Coming Charismatic Church, with a black bulletin board out front advertising three services come Sunday morning. Not to mention one on Sunday night, which Reverend Holiday had been quick to point out. Someone had gone to a lot of trouble to plant impatiens and wild roses—summer flowers—in a carefully tended bed at the base of the sign. The church bordered a residential neighborhood, and a row of red-brick houses passed by her car window, each with the same identical white trim and black iron mailbox. A few sported the Texas flag in the front yard, and for those feeling particularly patriotic, an American one as well.

She turned down the main thoroughfare and drove into the parking lot of the Enterprise Police Station. Once again, only a few cars occupied the lot. What with high school still in session, there wasn't much call for the policemen on a Tuesday morning. She picked a spot by the door and grabbed her purse, which held her trusty notebook, on her way out of the car. Through the glass doors and into the same dreary lobby she walked, with the FBI's most wanted staring at her from fading posters. This morning, Sergeant Hines stood beside a tidy counter that sported a coffeepot and a stack of foam cups. He noticed her right away.

"Morning, Miss Garrett. You're just in time for some coffee." He motioned to the carafe in his hands.

She'd already had a cup at Bernie's, but a second wouldn't kill her. "Thanks. How about black?" She walked around the counter and approached the sergeant, accepting the cup he offered her.

"This makes twice in one week I've seen you," he told her as she drank from the warm cup. "People are going to start talking if we don't watch out."

She pursed her lips against the bitter taste. "That seems to be a hobby around here, anyway. Do you have a moment, Sergeant?" She glanced around the empty room, thankful for the silence.

"Of course." Sergeant Hines waved toward his desk, up against the wall. For the first time, she noticed a large mirror mounted to the ceiling, angled toward his desk.

"Expecting a gunfight?" She nodded toward the mirror.

"You like that, huh? Figure it's best to see people coming and going. By the way, you've got a spot on the back of your skirt."

She twisted around and saw a minute stain on the skirt's hem. "Not much gets by you, does it?" She twisted around to face him again. "That's why I knew you'd be the right person to ask about something."

"Do tell." Slowly, he stirred his coffee as he spoke, the black liquid sludging from side to side.

"LilliFay Holiday came to the *Country Caller* this morning.

You should have seen her . . . I couldn't believe her get-up."

"The purple hat, huh? Seems to be her calling card." The sergeant smiled to himself as he continued to work the coffee. She noticed he never actually drank it.

"It was odd, but she brought up Park Daniels. Do you know him?" she asked. "LilliFay seems to think Becca Cooper's death had something to do with him."

"Park, huh? Now, why would she think that?" Finally, the sergeant took a sip from the cup, his eyes narrowing.

"That's what I wanted to know." Kelsey shrugged her shoulders, as if the news didn't mean that much to her.

"Not that he isn't a fine-looking young man. Gets that from my side of the family."

Kelsey blinked. "Come again?"

"He's my nephew, Miss Garrett. Real good boy. He and Becca dated a while back, but it fell apart pretty quick. Guess he figured he couldn't compete with the good reverend." Sergeant Hines motioned toward his desk, and they both settled into their respective chairs. "Thing I have to ask myself is, why did LilliFay feel the need to share the bit about Park and Becca with you?"

"That's what I want to know." Her eyes swept the wall behind his head. The calendar, with its angry red tick marks, was gone. "Where's the calendar, sergeant? You're not planning on going anywhere, are you?" She studied the desktop now. Quite a few things seemed to be missing. Where was the messy pile of file folders, spilling to the edge of the desk? The discarded potato chip bags and leftover gum wrappers? The plastic ashtray stuffed with quarters for the soda machine? The only thing that remained was the deer head, still marooned on the wall. Everything else seemed to have vanished.

"Oh, that. Remember how I was all set to retire?" He inhaled deeply, then exhaled. "Turns out today's the day. My pension plan says you can't work a day over your fifth year in it. It's called the deferred option retirement plan. Now I have to up and leave. That's just how it works."

The space seemed so barren now. Sterile, actually. "Rules say I have to formally retire now," he continued. "It's a gift they give you after twenty-five years with the force, that five-year pension thing. According to the payroll department, I'm no longer on active service, Miss Garrett."

"But what about Miss Cooper's death? The investigation?" Her voice trailed off helplessly. Never did she expect to have to work this story on her own. She'd assumed Sergeant Hines would be right beside her, ferreting out clues and talking through the information he'd found.

"It doesn't mean I'm dropping the case," he insisted. "Nothing like this has happened in Enterprise in a long time, and I won't just walk away. A deputy will be working leads, and there are always the detectives from Houston, but I'll be right there, too."

"I see." Only, she didn't quite believe things would stay the same if Sergeant Hines wasn't an active member of the police force. Her job would be more difficult, no doubt about that. Perhaps impossible. If she couldn't find out who was being interrogated and why, she'd have to work leads all on her own. Truth be told, she'd also miss his company along the way. "Promise you won't just disappear?" She watched him carefully, gauging his reaction.

"How could I do that? There's my nephew to consider. He's got as much at stake in finding the person who killed Becca Cooper as anybody."

"Really?" That statement hung awkwardly in the air between them. Before he could answer, the door jangled open and Earline bustled in, fired up about something or other. The mood now broken, they both fell silent.

CHAPTER 11

Hiding behind the safety of the enormous purple hat, LilliFay peeked up to survey the parking lot of Second Coming Charismatic Church. In front of her sat a black and white squad car, glinting angrily in the late-morning sun.

Honestly . . . how were people ever going to get over this tragedy if the police kept showing up on the church's doorstep? The hunk of black and white metal looked so ugly next to the flower bed she'd taken great pains to plant, and the beige bricks she made sure got power-washed every month whether they needed it or not.

She scurried around the squad car and ducked into the hallway of the administrative offices. Cool air conditioning blew against her neck and arms, much better than the stuffy newsroom she'd come from. That young reporter seemed nice enough, but if she and Bobby were ever going to make this thing work, LilliFay would have to be certain no one linked Bobby with Becca Cooper's murder. As far as anyone was concerned, Bobby had come home that night right on time, early even, and stayed in that house with her until the sun reappeared in the east. That was her story, so help her God.

She picked up her pace in the hallway after spying Velma at the end of it. She figured she might as well make herself useful, and Bobby could surely use some help packing up his office. What with thirty years' worth of books and all of the knick-knacks church members insisted on giving him . . . not that he kept all of them, but there were enough homemade doilies and wooden bookends to give him a hernia if he didn't watch out. The least she could do was lend a hand.

Halfway there, she noticed Velma wasn't alone. When the woman leaned away from the wall, Davey, one of the younger members of the police force, appeared. What were the chances? That officer would never let LilliFay be until she'd answered a thousand questions about what she was doing at the church, so LilliFay turned on her heel and began to backtrack the way she'd come.

Thankfully, Velma and Davey were so busy chit-chatting, they didn't even notice her come and go down the very same hall. *Now what?* It wasn't like she could fly into Bobby's office un-noticed, not with those two guarding the door to it.

Once out in the parking lot again, LilliFay paused beside the squad car. Sunshine bounced off the front window, causing her to squint. There had to be another way.

Actually . . . she snapped her fingers, which wasn't easy considering the Sunday gloves and all. Didn't Bobby tell her about a back door once, and how it was the only way he could leave sometimes without being stopped by everybody and their cousin for a handshake after the service? He called it his "escape hatch." Said he felt like a magician coming and going through a secret passageway hidden to everybody else. That was how she could reach Bobby. Without the young police officer ever suspecting a thing.

In no time at all, LilliFay found the hidden door, stuck behind an overgrown azalea bush. It'd been recessed into the brick wall, with only a tiny keyhole placed discreetly to the side to distinguish it as a door. Whatever else she might say about Park Daniels and his handiwork, he surely knew how to build a secret door. She pressed her fingers against the warm wood and slid it to the right—no need for the key even. It was dark inside, so she peered into the space before stepping over the transom.

Oh, but it was dark. The bottom of her pump caught the edge of the transom and she almost sprawled headfirst through the panel. At the last second, she braced her palm against the wall and stood teetering over the indoor-outdoor carpet. Before righting herself, she glimpsed something white and round and rumpled lying on the carpet. Not quite round, though, more like a sphere that'd been crumpled and crushed.

She reached for the orb and flattened it against her palm as she righted herself. Maybe it was one of Bobby's sermon notes. The few times he left behind a scrap of paper, she'd squirreled it away to add to his scrapbook, for later. Such a modest man. Some of his words should be saved for posterity, and she was the one to do it.

She angled the page toward the daylight. This one was much too brief to be a sermon note, and it had been typed, not handwritten in permanent ink, like her Bobby would do.

The paper was addressed to Becca Cooper, of all people. Whatever she held in her hand, it was highly personal and highly private, and her eyes flew to the next line.

I'll never forgive you for leaving. You'll be sorry.

What in the world? LilliFay cocked her head as she reread the note once, twice, three times . . . just to be safe. Whatever could the writer mean, she'd be sorry? There was no signature; no hint to the writer's identity. It could have come from anyone, really. Well, anyone with access to the passageway, that was.

LilliFay folded the note carefully and slipped it into her pocketbook. What to do? At a time like this she'd normally go to Bobby for his opinion, but after his little adventure the other night, she wasn't so sure. What if Bobby typed the note? She shook her head vehemently. No, that couldn't be right. Bobby hated word processors. Always had. At least, that's what he'd told her. No matter what, she'd have to commit herself to either visiting his office or leaving without a word. Which wouldn't get her any closer to the truth. She gazed pensively down the passageway before making up her mind.

By the time she reached Bobby's office it looked like he'd been there a while, surrounded by piles of books and all. He glanced her way when she came in, then looked again like he couldn't really be sure he'd seen her.

"You're looking mighty fancy," he told her.

"Figured I might as well dress up. No need to look all poor and pitiful." She laid her pocketbook on a closed moving box, withdrawing the crumpled note at the same time. "Found this today." She offered it to him without another word. Best to let him explain himself.

"What's that?" He gave the paper only a passing glance. He continued to pack as he spoke, placing books four at a time—a little haphazardly for her taste—into a different cardboard box. Apparently he'd saved the bookcase for last, because the rest of the room looked picked clean. Even the tissue boxes, which he'd placed around the room for his more emotional visitors, were gone.

"Here. Look at it." She thrust it out farther, encouraging him to pause. He finally laid down the books and reached for the piece of paper. "Let me do that," she said as she reached for the books in his hands. Bobby never did know how to pack, not properly. Large books on the bottom, paperbacks on top. Everybody knew that. She set about filling the box, keeping her eyes focused on the task at hand.

Bobby inhaled sharply once he read the note, a sucking sound that filled the room. Either he'd never seen it, or he never expected to see it again. "What's this, LilliFay?" He seemed genuinely surprised by the paper he held in his hand. Surprised and saddened.

"I found that on the floor. Something, isn't it?" The paper

stood between them like a barricade neither was willing to breach.

"You should give this to the police," he finally said. Only then did he lay the sheet on top of the box, gently. "It belongs with them." His surprise at seeing the note—that she'd expected. The sadness, not really. If she didn't know better, she'd think he was about to break down and cry.

"What is it, Bobby? What does it mean?" She spoke quietly, afraid to hear the answer but desperate for an explanation that made sense.

"She must've had a boyfriend, LilliFay. That's all. Can't say I'm shocked." With that, he turned to face the nearly empty bookcase, hiding his emotions from her really.

"So you didn't write the note?"

His shoulders sagged even lower. She hadn't meant to upset him, but she'd found something important; she knew that. Usually, he was the one with the big news; he had the dramatic statements. Not her.

"No, it's not from me. I wouldn't write that." He refused to turn around, forcing her to watch him from behind. "You should have known that right away."

Truth be told, she did know that. No matter what else her Bobby was, and heaven only knew he could be as stubborn as the next man, he wasn't violent. He would never hurt anyone. Violence wasn't in him.

"Where did you go the other night, Bobby?" There, alone in the vanishing study, with nothing but the sound of far-off whirs from the street outside, it seemed as good a time as any to ask the question. "You didn't come home until sunup, and that was the night she died."

That did it. Finally, Bobby turned around to face her. He had been hiding, after all, probably ashamed of the tear that streaked down his cheek. A single tear, running from temple to chin.

"I fell asleep here," he said, pointing to the desk. "Spent half the night working on my sermon. If people only knew . . ." his voice trailed off.

Wordlessly, she walked to where he stood. Held out her arms and tenderly wrapped them around his shoulders. Held him closer than she'd ever held him before.

Yes, she should have known. No matter what, Bobby was still her sanctuary. Bobby would always be her home.

Kelsey rifled through her closet before Park arrived for their date, looking for something a little sexy, but a little innocent, too. She'd only seen him twice, and both times she'd been dressed for work, so she needed to show him her other side; the fun side.

She settled on a ruffled yellow shirt and blue-jean miniskirt, which was a little casual, but he didn't seem the fancy type. By the time she changed and brushed her hair—again—it was nearly seven o'clock, so she yelped and flew down the stairs. After sweeping a few dirty mugs into the dishwasher and running a sponge over the linoleum counter, she stepped back to appraise the scene. Not bad. The kitchen was a little cluttered, but homey. Comfortable, even. She moved to the living room to straighten a pile of unread magazines, when an engine revved outside.

At the last moment, she smiled at herself in the hall mirror before moving to the front door, an old trick of hers from high school. Any time she felt uneasy, she'd pretend she was a supermodel on a photo shoot and a photographer lurked just past the mirror. Silly, wasn't it? But it seemed to work, because she opened the door with gusto, and there was Park . . . standing on the landing with something hidden behind his back.

"For you." He grinned and withdrew a bunch of tulips from their hiding spot.

"They're beautiful!" She accepted the flowers, and pressed her face into their fragrant blooms. "How did you know?" Dutch tulips were her favorite, and purple ones, yet. She hadn't told a soul since she moved to Enterprise.

"The gal at the flower stand said you buy them all the time." He patiently waited while she inhaled the perfume. "Said you're the only one in Enterprise who does." He pointed to the inside of the house. "Mind if I come in?"

Finally, she looked up. "What? Of course. Come on in. And thank you." She waved him in, cradling the bouquet carefully in her other arm. "Let me put these in water before we go."

He stepped over the landing with her, and followed her into the kitchen. "Say, this place looks a lot better. What'd you do to it?"

She shrugged as she rummaged around in a cabinet for a suitable vase. "A little bleach, a little elbow grease. Nothing here a good cleaning wouldn't help." She pulled out a mason jar and held it under the faucet as she spoke. "I like fixing things."

He watched her as water rose to the top of the jar; she could feel his eyes on the back of her neck. "We're two peas in a pod. I've actually done some work at this place, off and on. That staircase wasn't nothing but a pile of matchsticks before you got here."

She giggled and set the jar on the countertop. "Wasn't nothing? You are *so* southern." When his smile fell, she rushed to add, "I mean, it's fun. I wish my accent was as strong as yours."

The grin returned to his face, thankfully. "We can't help it if you Yankees up in Houston talk funny." He sat at the table, still watching her. "I figure as long as I get my point across, that's all that counts."

112

She joined him at the table, conscious of his now-empty hands. "Can I get you a beer? I've got ambers, lights, you name it. Say the word."

"I'm good. We might want to get something at the restaurant. That is, if you're still fixin' to go with me." His eyes twinkled merrily.

"Don't you start." She swatted at him. "We'll be here all night if I took to fixin' your grammar." His tanned cheeks played up his sunny smile brilliantly. Before, she'd been too taken with his eyes to notice much else about his features. Now that she saw him up close, she could see the resemblance to Sergeant Hines. The strong jaw, the same nose; definitely part of the same family. "Hey, I ran into your uncle at the police station the other day."

Park leaned back in his chair casually. "That so? How is Uncle George?"

"Good. He's good." The back of the police station had been swept clean the last time she saw him. "Course, I didn't know he was leaving the police department so soon. I was kind of hoping he'd wait until after this investigation is over."

"Say, maybe I'll have that beer after all."

She tilted her head to the side in lieu of answering. Funny how his tone had changed so suddenly, from teasing to serious. "Okay." She rose to retrieve a bottle from the refrigerator. "Did you know he was retiring?"

"Yeah, we all did. He has to, if he wants to keep his pension. He won't let this thing rest, though. Not until they find out who killed Becca Cooper."

She brought the beer to the table, watching him all the while. He didn't seem particularly uncomfortable, more like sad. "He says you knew her." Still no reaction, other than accepting the bottle from her and twisting off the cap. The metal plinked to the tabletop.

"We dated for a while. That was some gal." He shook his head before bringing the beer to his lips. After a quick swallow, he continued, "Did you know she used to play piano at the old folks home? She wouldn't take a dime for it, neither. She loved those grandmas and grandpas."

"So, why'd you break up with her?" Though the question seemed a little abrupt, she'd been wondering about that for awhile now.

"We wanted different things. Okay . . . why the sudden interest in Becca Cooper? For the newspaper, I'm guessing."

Now it was her turn to shake her head. "Not just that. Even if I wasn't doing the feature stories, I'd want to know. People don't die every day in a small town like this. But nobody wants to say too much." It was true. Beyond Sergeant Hines and a quirky visit from LilliFay Holiday, getting the locals to talk was nearly impossible, she'd found. They draped a cloak of silence around them whenever she approached.

"That's because most of us are family. You don't talk about family with strangers." He took another gulp from his beer, his fingers smudging some oval prints left behind from the first drink.

"Is that what I am? A stranger? Just because I wasn't born here doesn't mean I don't care. The girl was murdered, for goodness sake."

"Look, can we talk about something else for a while?" He seemed exasperated by their conversation now.

"I guess. I find it interesting, that's all. Sergeant Hines—Uncle George—says he may have a suspect."

"Really? Who?"

"He's not saying. Not yet, anyway." Sergeant Hines hadn't said anything of the sort, but it must be true. Half a week had passed since Becca's body was found in the bayou, which was a lifetime in police work. She knew the longer an investigation went without a suspect being found, the more likely it would never be solved.

"I hope they find him. Or her," Park said. "Becca wasn't always smart about the way she lived her life, but that was her business."

"Well . . . who do you think did it?" There. Nothing like asking outright. As her editor always said, if you don't ask, you don't get.

"Well, I'll tell you who didn't do it." He wrapped his fingers around the bottle tightly. Laced them together until the color started to drain from the tips. "I don't think Reverend Holiday killed her, that's for sure. He wouldn't hurt anyone. Not from what I'd seen. More likely it was someone from out of town. People think one of us had to be involved, but maybe not."

What did he mean, us? She knew Park and Becca had dated casually, as much as she knew Becca Cooper had had at least one other boyfriend.

"I mean, it could have been anyone, right?" He unlaced his fingers and pushed the bottle away. "Come on, Kelsey, it's time to get some food in your stomach and stop all this speculating. Let the police do their job. They'll have an answer soon enough."

She watched him rise from the table, more confused than ever. She'd never thought about someone from outside of town being the killer. And, didn't Park just admit the locals had a hard time trusting anyone who wasn't from Enterprise? Why should Becca Cooper be any different?

He stood behind her chair now, slowly pulling it away from the table to help her to her feet. Come to think of, Becca had been an outsider, too. Just like her. She'd lived in Enterprise for only a few years, leaving her family and friends behind in Oklahoma, while Kelsey had left everyone she knew behind in Houston to take the job at the *Country Caller*.

Reluctantly, she rose. The more she thought about it, she had a lot in common with Becca Cooper. Including the fact that both of them had gone out with Park Daniels.

"Are you chilly?" he softly asked. "You shivered."

"No." She turned and smiled at him. "Must be the air conditioning. Maybe I'll have you check on that sometime."

They left the cottage in silence and arrived at the restaurant in a minute or two. It was a low, squat building with an outdoor patio and a stone fountain in front. Rumor had it this was the nicest restaurant in town, or did Renee once say it was the only nice restaurant in town? Hard to know since she'd never been inside herself.

One time, though, as she passed the place on a Friday night, she saw teenaged couples holding hands by the fountain, dressed in their best prom wear, so the rumor must be true.

Park swerved the pickup into a parking space, then ran to her side of the truck before she could open her own door. He swung it wide and made a sweeping gesture with his hand. "Only the finest," he told her as he took her hand and helped her from the cab to the gravel parking lot.

The minute they entered the door, Kelsey felt as if she was on display. The young hostess who greeted them at the door took one look at her and Park together and sighed. She looked especially disappointed when Park asked for a table for two, then mentioned he'd already reserved a space on the back patio. As they followed the pouting girl through the restaurant—which was softly lit by candles and reflected light from a crystal chandelier—she heard whispers, which she did her best to ignore. She followed the girl through a back door and onto a patio, where a shower of lights twinkled from a magnificent willow. It looked as if the tree had been set afire and flames licked at its outer branches.

"So lovely," Kelsey whispered, as the hostess pulled out a chair from a back table, near the patio rail. The sound of water trickled over stones at their feet, the edge of a stream that meandered under the patio. Overhead, the lights blinked in unison.

"Nothing but the best." Park took over from the hostess and helped her settle into the chair. The girl disappeared after giving them each a menu.

"Come here often, I take it?"

"Only once or twice. Know that little girl from church." He studied the wine menu as he spoke. Kelsey figured he must be talking about the hostess.

"May I ask you something?" Might as well get her questions out in the open right off the bat. "Were you and Becca Cooper, you know . . ." She struggled to find the right words.

Instead of answering her, he lowered the wine menu. He looked amused. "Dating? Good friends? Lovers?"

"Bingo." She exhaled. "Take your pick. Do any of the above fit?"

"A gentleman doesn't kiss and tell, Kelsey."

"Oh. Right." She must have looked as deflated as she felt, because he reached across the table and placed his palm under her chin. He drew her face up until they were eye-to-eye again.

"But, so you know . . . our relationship wasn't that serious. And I never took her here. Not once."

"In that case, I'd love a glass of wine." The strung lights seemed to blink even brighter now that she'd cleared the air. Pictures in the newspaper aside, maybe it had been a summer fling or a one-week romance that flickered out before it could burn too bright. Either way, no ghosts of former girlfriends would haunt them on the patio that night, so she might as well loosen up and enjoy herself. Heaven only knew she had earned one night to relax. One night to be herself.

When a waitress appeared, they both ordered the special of the house, and Kelsey settled in for conversation and privacy.

Here, on the back patio, under the canopy of pin lights and black sky, she could finally relax.

They spoke of little things at first. Family histories, favorite pastimes, that kind of thing. Turns out Park had a secret weakness for the Dallas football team, which was almost heresy in this part of Texas, and driving his pickup off-road on Sunday afternoons. He started to tell her a story about getting stuck in a ravine, when an older woman appeared next to him at their table, her face flushed.

"Excuse me." She spat the words out. "You're Kelsey Garrett, aren't you?" She ignored Park as she spoke.

"Hello, Miss Bertha." Park rose from the table and laid his napkin on his plate. "Where's Winslow?"

"He's in the restroom right now. It's our thirtieth, you know." Her tone warmed as she turned to Park. "That man surprised me after all these years. Got me the prime rib, too. It's my favorite." The warmth disappeared as she remembered why she had walked onto the back patio, after all. "I'm here to talk to your date, Park. This has nothing to do with you."

Kelsey laid her fork down. "May I help you, ma'am?" Whatever it was the woman had come to say, it didn't sound like good news. Maybe Kelsey had misspelled someone's name in the newspaper, or maybe the delivery person was a bad aim, or hadn't shown up at all.

"Yes, yes you can help me." She seemed to be about sixty, with white hair and pearl earrings big as buttons. Dressed for a night on the town, all right. "You need to stop writing those stories about that poor dead girl. It's not right to make money off of someone's misfortune."

"Well." Now it was Kelsey's turn to rise from the table. Damned if she'd let a perfect stranger interrupt their date. "It's an important story, and people have the right to know about it."

"We don't work that way. Maybe it's okay back where you come from, but it's not okay here. The Holidays are like family to us."

So that's what this was about. Not that she had dared to write a news feature about the disappearance, then murder, of a local girl, but that she had dared to name the minister and his wife as suspects. Kelsey rolled her shoulders back. "I don't care if the Queen of England had something to do with it. We report the facts. It's our job. We treat everyone the same."

The woman's jaw dropped open. When she finally spoke, she directed her words at Park. "Are you gonna let her talk to me like that? Honestly, Park Daniels, if you can't find someone better to date, maybe I should speak to your uncle!" She stormed off, the slap of her heels against wood echoing in the night.

Park chuckled and sank into his chair. "Don't that beat all."

Kelsey shrugged, more rattled than she cared to admit. "What was that all about?"

"Seems you've riled up Miss Bertha. No doubt Winslow, too." Sensing her confusion, he reached across the table and took her hand in his. "Don't think twice. Lots of folks here have nothing better to do than to stir up trouble. If it wasn't you, she'd have found something else to go off about."

"You sure?" The woman sounded so angry. Enraged, even. "She was really mad."

"Look . . . you were doing your job, like you said. Don't let her scare you. Half the time people here say something and forget about it by morning. Can't let it bother you."

Easy for him to say. He'd spent his whole life in Enterprise, getting used to its quirks. She'd only been in town six months and already one woman looked ready to strike her.

"Something from the wine menu?" The waitress had returned to their table.

"Definitely." Kelsey glanced at Park. "A bottle of anything, please."

The next day dawned hot and bright as Kelsey left her house for the day. Late, of course, since her date with Park had lasted until well after midnight. When he finally dropped her off at the front door, leaving her breathless with one last kiss, she replayed the scene over and over in her mind for another hour until sleep finally came.

It was worth it, though. She hummed as she drove her car into the parking lot of the Enterprise police station. Definitely worth it. While Park wasn't too eager to talk about Becca Cooper's murder, he did make her laugh with story after story. Except for having to listen to Bertha, the hostile woman with the sour face, their date had been picture-perfect.

Which was all well and good, but now that sunlight breached the horizon, it was time to focus. By the end of the day, Renee would be clamoring for new information, and Kelsey would have to give it to her if she wanted to keep up with her newspaper series.

Thankfully, she saw Sergeant Hines by the coffee pot again when she entered the police station. He looked tired, too. It must be something that was going around.

"Morning, Sergeant. Any left for me?"

He handed her a crackled mug bearing the logo of the Enterprise Chamber of Commerce. "Feeling brave today, are we?" he asked. Steam seeped from the cup as he poured remnants of the pot into it. "Glad you came by today. I just stopped in to pick up some mail and I got something you might find interesting."

"Really?" She followed him back to his desk, which was bare save for a lone plastic baggie.

"Someone left this at the station last night." Sergeant Hines smoothed the plastic bag with his free hand, flattening a paper sealed inside it. "It was addressed to Becca Cooper. Here." He swiveled the bag around to face her, then began to read aloud from the sheet inside. *"I'll never forgive you for leaving. You'll be sorry."*

She stared at the evidence. Typewritten, crumpled, the paper looked innocuous enough under the station's harsh fluorescent lights. Except for the fact that it'd been addressed to a girl who was no longer alive. "What do you think it means?"

The sergeant tapped the bag with his finger. "I think our Miss Cooper made someone very mad. Maybe mad enough to kill her."

Kelsey set the mug in her hand aside, forgetting all about the cooling coffee. "Sounds like a man wrote it. But you never know. "

"I'd say you're right. Sounds like she left someone and he didn't take it too kindly. Now, where does that leave us?"

"It leaves us with several suspects," Kelsey replied. The image of Park standing on her walkway with delicate tulips in his hand nagged at her. "Anyone who dated Becca Cooper."

"Bingo." The sergeant finally took a drink from his mug. A long drink, as if working through a mental checklist at the same time. "Truth be told, one of our main suspects—a woman—has a solid alibi for the morning Becca Cooper died."

Kelsey reread the note slowly. Not only had someone tried to destroy the note, but someone else had left it at the police station for the sergeant to find. Both facts held intriguing possibilities.

"First thing I did was run checks on LilliFay Holiday," he said. "Now, we all know she's a little eccentric, but could she have murdered Becca Cooper? I doubt it, but stranger things have happened."

"Oh?"

"She comes up clean. Said she was home Friday morning, watching a television shopping network."

"That doesn't mean she didn't have time to leave her house in between shows," Kelsey said.

The sergeant held his coffee cup steadily, chest high. "She bought a few things over the course of several hours. Got the records from the network. There's no way LilliFay would have time to shop, then make it out to meet Becca. The coroner's placing the time of death at around eight o'clock, right when LilliFay bought a cowl-neck tunic, whatever that is."

Kelsey groaned softly. One suspect down, several more to go. "Did the coroner's report say anything else?"

"Just what we already knew . . . the victim was four months pregnant, and she'd been whacked on the side of her head with a blunt object. Forcefully."

"What about the weapon. Any ideas?" She leaned forward now, the plastic bag looming large on the table.

"Not exactly. But for something to make that kind of a mark on a human skull, it had to have been heavy. Probably something you'd hold away from you, too."

"Why's that?" She knew enough about police procedure to know they'd analyze angles and placement, but she didn't expect them to be able to judge distance.

"People usually pick something that'll put space between them and the victim. Especially if they know 'em. It's psychological, Miss Garrett. The better you know a person, the more you want that distance."

"I see." Reluctantly, Kelsey tore her eyes away from the bag and checked her watch. Nine o'clock. Renee would be bustling through the doors of the newsroom right about now. "I have to leave, but I'd like to call you later. I need a quote for my story, if you don't mind."

Sergeant Hines set his coffee cup down, right next to the

evidence. "Don't mind at all. We're running out of time. I'd say we have another day or two and then it's all over."

She thanked him for his time and turned to leave. As she backed away from his desk and the note that lay in the plastic bubble, she almost ran into the counter. She cleared it at the last second, though, and managed to leave the police station with no further missteps.

Several bits of evidence tied to Becca Cooper's death had surfaced. Now it was time to link them until one solid picture emerged. After a few moments spent driving, Kelsey swerved onto Fifth Street and parked between the newsroom and the Grande Burrito. Even though Renee might be looking for her at that very moment, she had another, and more important, stop to make.

Bernie looked up from the cash register as she walked in. Today, he wore a guayabera shirt, of all things, for the first time trying to blend in with his surroundings. Even with the Mexican shirt, he still looked like a tanned St. Nick in flip-flops.

"Morning, Bernie." She picked the same table as the day before, which faced the window and a half-moon of Hawaiian fabric.

"The usual?" He started to draw back the serape as he spoke. This time, one other couple sat in the restaurant, near the ice machine in the back, but they paid her no mind as they huddled over their plates.

"You've got it. Heavy on the cheese again." She pulled out a rickety chair and sat down. Today, Jimmy Buffet had been replaced by Bob Marley, and the sound of Conga drums and reggae riffs played over the stereo speaker. While the rest of the world had discovered surround-sound, Bernie had mounted an old stereo speaker above the door and called it good. It fit in with a neon beer sign in the corner, though.

Kelsey smoothed down the paper placemat in front of her,

which did its best to be south of the border by adding a splash of yellow and red. Once again, a dusting of salt lay on the place-mat, and it glistened in the morning sun. "Your helper needs to step it up." She swept the crystals to the floor with her palm. "How's he working out for you?"

Although she had looked forward to another breakfast of eggs and caffeine, she was more interested in the stranger she saw at the restaurant yesterday. If Becca Cooper's ex-husband had moved to Enterprise, that would change everything. That would add the strongest suspect yet to the list . . . a list that had been whittled down by one now that LilliFay Holiday had her alibi with the Home Shopping Network.

Bernie emerged from behind the serape with a porcelain mug in his hand. He placed it on the table and pulled out the chair opposite hers. The beige guayabera shirt looked damp, even at this early hour, and his forehead was already moist from the humidity.

"That's another story." He threw up his hands. "I'm back to being a one-man band. Can you believe the guy left after one day?"

Kelsey ignored the coffee now cooling in the mug. "Why would he quit after one day?"

"That's what I'd like to know. First thing I did was check the cash register, but nothing's missing. If he wants to go and mess up his life like that, I guess it's his business." Bernie leaned back in his chair and laced his fingers behind his head. "He did seem like an odd duck to me. Kind of a mystery man."

"How so?" She hadn't caught but a glimpse of the stranger's sandy blond hair and weathered face. He walked with jerky mo-tions; that much she remembered, and he seemed to be in an awful hurry the day before.

"I don't know. I didn't get a good feeling from him. Like maybe there was more there." Bernie balanced the chair precariously as he spoke. A large man, his stomach protruded when he leaned further in the chair, straining the buttons on the guayabera almost to the breaking point.

"Then why'd you hire him?" It didn't make sense to offer a job to someone like that, at least not to her.

"I'm all about giving people second chances. If I didn't, who would?" His features softened. "The guy said he lost everything back home and didn't own anything but the shirt on his back. That's down on your luck."

"Hmmm." Finally, Kelsey lifted the coffee mug to her lips. After a long drink, she set it down again. "What if I told you the guy might be a fugitive?" Even though she had viewed the mug shot on her ancient computer screen, there was no mistaking the haunted look in the man's eyes, the drawn cast of his face.

"Hope not." Bernie rocked the chair forward until both legs touched the ground again. "Would hate to have helped someone like that. Though the most I gave him was a few burritos and a soda. He didn't stick around long enough to be paid. What do you think could have spooked him?"

From the corner of her eye, Kelsey noticed the couple near the back of the restaurant had gathered their things to leave. It must have been later than she thought. Renee could be searching for her at that very second, unaware she sat two doors down at a dusty table with a hot cup of coffee in her hand.

"I have no idea, Bernie. But I'm going to find out." She wasn't going to find out sitting in any restaurant, though. "Hold my order, will you? No time for breakfast today." She nodded toward the only other diners in the place. "Looks like your paying customers are ready to go, too." With that, she grabbed a few dollars from her pocket and laid them on the table. "Sorry about your worker. Who knows, he may show up again."

CHAPTER 12

Kelsey dashed from the restaurant to the newsroom in record time. So, LilliFay was no longer a suspect in Becca Cooper's murder, and the ex-husband—if that really was him—had disappeared. That still left a handful of strong suspects: Bobby Holiday; his ever-vigilant secretary, Velma; even Shawn Deschamps, the skinny teenager who found the body on the bayou; and—unfortunately—Park Daniels. She winced at the last thought. How could the man who held her so tenderly in his arms the night before have committed this crime? If she honestly thought he had anything to do with Becca Cooper's murder, she never would have gone out with him or let him grow close. Or, at least, she didn't think she would. What with those beautiful eyes and handsome features she didn't know what to think anymore.

Always, she considered herself to be a good judge of character. There would have been signs. Maybe an awkward pause. An eerie quirk or two. Even back in college, when a drunk classmate tried to coerce her into getting in the car with him, or a college advisor got a little too chummy, she'd always known what to do. Her survival instinct kicked in when something felt wrong, and nothing about the night before had felt wrong.

She swept into the newsroom. Surprisingly, Renee was nowhere to be found. Since their sports reporter worked nights, and the columnists and ad sales reps all worked freelance, she had the whole room to herself. What little there was of it: a few desks, a file cabinet or two, and her trusty computer screen taking root on a desk in the corner.

She dropped her purse to the floor and flicked on the computer. When she submitted her story to the newswire editor yesterday, he sounded surprisingly interested. Especially when she played up the small-town angle. Even though the wire service had its own beat reporters, she knew they'd be willing to take her story if she pitched it just right. Using her work would be a win-win for everyone: they'd get a story to send out to member newspapers, and she'd have another clipping for her portfolio. What could go wrong?

She logged onto the Houston daily's website with a few well-placed taps. As the home page slowly unfurled on her screen—the machine wasn't the fastest she'd ever used, but it got the job done—she searched for the local news icon at the top of the page. Why, what do you know . . . there it was, in the far left column, right after the home page. The headline—*Church Worker's Body Discovered In Bayou*—jumped off the screen, set in huge type that dwarfed the other stories. Or so it seemed to Kelsey. She chewed at her thumbnail as the pixels wavered on the glowing screen. It had worked. The editor had picked up on her story, bundled it to member newspapers, and there it was, for all to see. Only she didn't expect to feel so odd about seeing her words broadcast to one of the largest cities in Texas.

She leaned back. It wasn't what she'd expected, that was for sure. Not what she'd expected at all. She should have been overjoyed, not mortified. Especially when the faces of Bobby Holiday and Sergeant Hines began to dance around her computer screen, giving life to the dead words on the page. This wasn't just a story. This was Enterprise. This was real people, with a real death and real lives that hung in the balance. She hadn't expected to feel like covering the screen with her hands;

erasing the words from the web page. She continued to stare at the screen until the trill of her telephone yanked her out of her reverie. "Hello?"

A man's voice, thick and hoarse, came on the line. "You've gone too far."

Finally, she tore her eyes away from the screen. "Who is this?" She didn't recognize the speaker, and even if she had, his words didn't make sense.

"Stop with the stories . . . let it alone." The man sounded angry. Not just angry, but threatening. "You'll be sorry if you don't."

The newsroom began to warm. "Look, whoever you are—" Before she had time to continue, to let the caller have a piece of her mind, the line went dead.

Her fingers trembled as she replaced the telephone receiver. She'd never been threatened before, especially not by a stranger. One who had access to her direct telephone line, no less.

"Are you okay, Kelsey?" While she was preoccupied, the door must have opened, the sleigh bells probably chiming, and now Renee stood at her desk.

"Huh?" Little by little, everything came into focus. The whir of the printing press next door, the sound of traffic on Fifth Street, the worried look on Renee's face. "Yeah, I think so."

"You look like you've seen a ghost."

"Almost. I think I just had my first anonymous threat."

Renee gasped and walked around the desk to stand near her chair. "You're kidding! Tell me everything . . . don't leave anything out."

For the next fifteen minutes, Kelsey explained how the wire service had used her story, the way it appeared on another newspaper's website, the telephone call that followed. Everything. Even the way Sergeant Hines explained LilliFay Holiday's alibi and the shrinking list of suspects.

"You'll have to call the police," Renee said firmly. "Tell them exactly what you told me. If some lunatic thinks he can threaten you, he's got another think coming."

Kelsey nodded. Truth be told, she needed someone strong like Renee in her corner. The caller had threatened her, after all. Not the newspaper, not the wire service, but her. "Yes, I'll call Sergeant Hines."

"Better yet, why don't you take some time off?" Renee's face looked pinched. "Go home, get some rest. Forget about this jerk. Come back when you feel a little stronger. I'll take over."

"Do you mind?" The room still felt too warm; downright hot, even.

"Not at all. Now scoot."

Kelsey did as she was told. Grabbed her purse, collected a few press releases to read later, and flicked off the computer screen. If the caller had meant to spook her, he'd succeeded. Oh yeah, he'd succeeded. She left the newsroom without a glance back.

Bobby Holiday bent forward to inhale the scent of furniture polish rising from the back of a pew. Orange with a hint of pine cones. Funny how the little things meant so much now that it was time to say good-bye. The way the stained glass windows poured color onto the carpet when the sun hit it just so. The cool wood against his fingers as he caressed a pew. The squeak of his shoes against the floor. Most mornings, when he ascended to the pulpit, the Sunday crowd would be so silent he could've dropped one of LilliFay's hats down from the rafters and he would've heard it land. Her and those silly hats. Even the vision of LilliFay sitting in the front row, her face shadowed by a huge brim . . . he'd miss that, too.

And the music. Always the music. The way Becca hunched over the piano keys and stroked them so gently they'd gladly sing for her. Sometimes, he shut his eyes tightly to block out everything but the sound of the music rising to the heavens. So many memories.

He continued to walk down the aisle, alone but surrounded by ghosts. There was the altar where he'd given his first communion, some thirty years ago. My, but his hands had trembled over the bread and wine. The spot where they'd place a casket—big or small, plain or ornate. He'd always be the last to see the deceased's face when the lid closed. The threadbare spot where the Christmas tree rubbed against the carpet every December twenty-fourth.

He'd miss it all. By the time he reached the altar, he gradually realized he wasn't alone after all. Someone had slipped through a side entrance and stood watching him as he made his pilgrimage to the altar.

"Good morning, Harris." Harris must have come from his office, because he wore a plain white button-down with the insurance company's logo.

"Hello, Reverend." Even though it felt like nothing had changed, Harris didn't return his smile.

"Are you picking up something?" It really wasn't any of his business, but Bobby felt protective of the sanctuary. This was still his house to protect, for as long as they'd let him protect it.

"You might say that." Harris pointed to an empty spot by the piano, where Becca Cooper's piano bench had been. "I see they've taken some things away."

"Guess so. Sergeant Hines said they need some things for the investigation. Say, Harris, do you have a minute?"

Even though Harris was one of the deacons who had voted to remove him from the church, he couldn't stay angry at him. Truth be told, if he had found out one of his staff members had been unfaithful to his spouse, he'd have done the very same thing. After all, they were leaders in the church, so more was expected of them. He knew that. Knowledge didn't soften the blow, but it did help him deal with the anger.

"Sure, Bobby." Harris walked to the front row of the church and sat down.

"Do you think they'll ever forgive me?" Bobby leaned against the pulpit. His rock in so many ways.

"Who, Bobby? The congregation?" Harris looked confused. "I suspect so. Can't say anyone was all that surprised when they found out about you and Becca."

"Not surprised?" That didn't seem possible. All that time, he and Becca had been so careful to keep their affair private. They'd drive for hours just to get a little privacy, purposefully avoiding each other at church. It didn't seem possible that everyone would know.

"She was a looker, Bobby. Come on. You're only human." Harris grinned. "Half the men were jealous, truth be told. They just won't tell you that."

That was scant comfort at a time like this. Becca was gone, and a new pastor would soon stand in his place. A stranger who didn't know every chink in the bricks, every crack in the pavement, every warp in the pew backs, the way he did. "Were you jealous, Harris?"

The deacon didn't answer right away. When he did, his voice was soft. "It's time to move on, Bobby. What's done is done. Do you need help packing up that office of yours? No need for you to do it alone."

Bobby gave him a half-smile. "Thanks, but LilliFay came around. She even loaded up my books and papers, after all that I've done to her. Can't believe she hasn't left me by now."

"That's because you're head of the household. God gave Adam the woman so he could rule over her. Don't you forget that."

Bobby straightened. "But I owe her for all of this. If it takes

131

the rest of my life, I'm going to make it up to her."

"If I were you, I wouldn't let her know how you feel. No telling how she might try to take advantage of the situation."

Sunlight melted through the deep burgundy stained glass behind Harris's head, lightening everything to pink. "I'm sure going to miss this place, Harris." Truth be told, the sanctuary already felt different somehow. Empty. Without Becca's beautiful piano playing and LilliFay sitting in the front row, it couldn't be the same. Funny how a place could change because of who wasn't there to enjoy it. "Take care of her, will you?"

Harris squinted at him. "Who, Bobby? LilliFay?"

"No. The church. Promise me you'll take care of her."

"Of course. Any time you want to come and visit, give me a call. We'll set it up for you." He pointed to the empty spot in front of the piano. "Think the police are going to bring those things back? They belong to the church."

Bobby shrugged. "I suppose. They're still going through Becca's things."

"Say, could you lock the door on the way out? I'd hate for the police to wander in here any time they felt like it and take away half the church."

Bobby nodded. As long as he had a key to the church, things couldn't be too bad. He'd still have a tie to his home.

"Oh, and give your keys to Velma. She'll need them for the next person."

The words hung in the air, until finally Bobby found his voice. "I'll do that, Harris. I'll do that."

Kelsey nearly tripped over the curb as she was leaving the newsroom, unable to focus on anything but the telephone call from the anonymous stranger. She'd felt hate pulse through the telephone line. Whoever placed that call had every intention of following through on his threat if she didn't stop writing about the murder . . . that much she knew.

What to do? She'd already spent part of the morning with Sergeant Hines and wasn't anxious to return so soon to the police department. He'd have to know about the call, of course, but at the moment all she could think about was clearing her mind and catching her breath.

And, then . . . she imagined Park Daniels sitting at her kitchen table the night before. He'd been so confident, so strong. Exactly what she needed right now. She wasn't quite sure what an agricultural pilot would be doing at ten o'clock on a Wednesday morning, but she wanted to find out. Quickly, she pulled out her cell phone and dialed the number he'd put there the night before. She fanned herself with her other hand as she waited for him to come on the line. The air felt leaden, dense with humidity. Summer was upon them, and the sultriness would stay for at least four months now. Four long months.

"Hello?"

"Park." She felt the quivering in her chest still. "Are you busy?"

"Working on a plane, Kelsey. Have to keep 'em in shape. What's up?"

Where to begin? "Something happened this morning." She was afraid she'd burst into tears if she said more.

"You okay? Where are you?" His words sounded rushed, worried.

"I'm going home. Can you meet me there?"

"You've got it." She noticed he didn't ask any questions, and he didn't put up any excuses. Two sentences from her, and he was willing to drop everything and rush to her side.

"Thank you." She flipped the phone closed and inhaled deeply. The answer had come to her as she stood on the hot pavement in front of the newsroom. Out of the blue, she'd realized there was only one person she wanted to see. When had that started? Before last night, Park was a stranger she'd run into at church by accident, and now his was the first name she thought of. She grew more relaxed as she drove home along Fifth Street, thankful to be putting some distance between her and the ominous black telephone back in the newsroom.

Fifteen minutes later, Park's truck pulled into her driveway. Just like that, he was in her kitchen, the look on his face a mix of anger and concern.

"Who would call you like that?" he asked, once she told him the story. He looked disgusted. Anonymous threats obviously violated every rule of manhood he held dear.

"That's the thing. I don't know, Park. I couldn't make out the voice. It all happened so fast." Her own voice softened. She couldn't even peg the speaker's age, not really. By the time he hung up, it was all a blur. She glanced at the empty coffee pot. "Where are my manners? I should offer you some coffee—"

"Don't worry about that." He waved off the suggestion. "We've got more important things to do." His fingers began to drum the breakfast table, just as his uncle's had drummed his desk at the police station. Must be a family habit.

After a moment, he said, "What if you quit writing the stories?"

Even though she'd turned to him first, there was still a lot about her he didn't know. "No way. This just makes me want to find out more. Everything I can." While she'd never actually been threatened before, she'd come across her share of hostile interview subjects. Usually, though, they tried to do an end-run around her by calling the managing editor or publisher to complain. They would never challenge her face-to-face. One thing she couldn't—or wouldn't—do was see this creep get what he wanted.

"Good for you, Kelsey."

Her shoulders relaxed even more. His praise sounded nice. *Very nice.*

"Question is, what do we do now?" Park continued to drum his fingers against the table. "We could call my uncle, or even go over there."

"I was there this morning. I'd hate to bother him again. He's going to get sick of me if I don't watch out."

"That's impossible. Who could get sick of seeing you?" He leaned forward protectively. "Don't worry, I won't leave you alone. You need a bodyguard, and I'm your man."

She liked the sound of that, too. "Thanks. There is one thing I wouldn't mind doing." She leaned closer to him, too, pulled by the feel of him. "I never got to see the place where they found Becca Cooper's body."

"Hmmm. Well, we can fix that. My uncle told me about it. Said it was on the bayou out back of Mason's Garage. Shouldn't be too hard to find."

"Do you mind?" So far, everything she'd heard about Becca Cooper's death had come secondhand, whether by talking with Sergeant Hines, or LilliFay Holiday, or visiting Second Coming Charismatic Church. She hadn't seen anything firsthand throughout this whole ordeal, which made her feel even more like an outsider, as if she were watching the scene from behind a filmy window. "I think if I see where it happened, it'll start to make more sense."

"Say no more." With that, he took her hand and together they rose from the table. "We can take my truck. If you don't mind riding with a toolbox and a Remington."

"Why in the world do you carry a gun?" Heaven only knew that everyone in Enterprise seemed to have a shotgun hanging in their pickup, so she shouldn't have been too surprised.

"Wouldn't be a Texan if I didn't have my gun. Come on."

He led her out of the kitchen and onto the porch in front of her house. He stopped there, under the porch light, and gave her a quick kiss, just like the night before. He smelled like motor oil and Dial soap. Earthy, but nice.

They drove in silence to the bayou behind Mason's Garage, listening to three George Strait songs in a row. She worked up the nerve to sing along on the last one. Park had a low, gravelly voice; lower than she'd expected. What with the wind rushing through the cab, it was hard to hear much of anything, so she felt free to belt out the song. They reached the bayou just as George finished pledging his love to someone without end, amen.

The bayou was deserted, save for clumps of reeds and wildflowers that edged the ravine, clinging to the last shreds of spring color. Blues faded to gray, vibrant pinks mellowed to rose, but they still provided some visual relief from the bright sun and stillness. Up ahead, Kelsey saw yellow caution tape strung between two weathered sawhorses. Working in a rectangle, police had stretched tape from the water's edge to a walking path above it. She pointed the tape out to Park, but there was no need.

"Why don't we call Sergeant Hines and have him meet us here?" Everything looked so official, cordoned off like that, and stark, compared to the natural surroundings. The last thing she wanted to do was disturb the crime scene of an ongoing investigation.

"Good idea. He'll come." Park withdrew his cell phone, dialed the number, and after saying a few words, slapped it shut again. "He'll be here in five."

"Do the men in your family always respond so fast?"

"It's all about taking care of the women. We hate to see a girl in trouble."

She smiled and took his hand, not waiting for him to make the first move. They began to walk along the dirt path, drawing near to the taped-off area. Aside from a few fire ant hills, everything looked flat and sparse and still. "I can't see anything unusual."

"Hmmm." Park stopped, and bent to examine something on the ground. He pointed to a piece of tissue paper lying there, thin as rice paper. "The police tried to lift some prints, but probably gave up. There aren't any flat surfaces here and nothing shiny, that's for sure."

They resumed walking. Once they reached the cordoned-off area, she saw a patch of reeds smashed against the dirt and two distinct ruts that ran from the bayou to the path. Like bicycle tracks, only broader and more shallow.

"They dragged her up here," Park said, and this time he pointed to the tracks. "She was probably bare-footed, from what I can tell."

Kelsey squinted. "Really?"

"Marks would've been deeper if she'd worn heels."

"How do you know things like that?" He seemed to understand an awful lot about crime scene investigations. More than she would have thought.

"I used to go on ride-alongs with my uncle. Probably got in the way more than anything else, but he tried to teach me a few things."

"Interesting." She had yet to see anything unusual, other than the drag marks in the dirt. "Shouldn't there be dust or something on the plants, from where they checked for fingerprints?"

Park shook his head. "There aren't any flat surfaces here, either. They probably combed the area and lifted anything they could find with tweezers. Hairs, threads, that kind of thing. The evidence would be long gone by now." At this point Park frowned. "Course, here in a bayou there's always animals to think of, too. Whatever the detective didn't find was probably carried off by the river rats."

Kelsey's eyes widened. "You're kidding! They actually have those?"

"Yeah, city girl. We call them nutria, but either way, they're nothing more than rats."

She shuddered, hoping to shake off the image he'd painted. "What if we walk around the edges, then? Maybe the investigators left something behind."

"Let's go that way." He pointed straight ahead, to the south. The path meandered a bit, but all in all it followed the flow of the bayou.

Seeing the drag marks had brought Becca's death closer, made it more real. It couldn't be abstract there on the bayou, with proof staring them in the face. "Do you ever think about her?" Now seemed as good a time as any to bring the old relationship up. He hadn't talked about his relationship with Becca before, not really.

"Sometimes. She was a great gal, Kelsey. Just a little messed up. She never should have gotten involved with the reverend."

Kelsey watched his face as he spoke. Usually, she could tell more about a person by what they didn't say than by what they said. That skill paid off in her line of work, and seemed to make people want to open up to her. Half the time she thought people were just grateful someone cared about what they had to say.

Park paused by a clump of bluebonnets, half the petals already shed on the ground. "She was kinda like this flower. Pretty, but fragile. I think she wanted someone to hold on to and didn't particularly care who. It could have been me, it could've been Bobby Holiday, it could've been anyone, really."

Kelsey took in the flower. Park sounded wistful, as if the girl were still alive and might join them on the bayou at any minute.

"I told her to leave him and she finally did. Doesn't much matter now, does it? You can't save someone like that. They have to make their own mistakes."

"Do you think he killed her?" Kelsey leveled her gaze at Park.

"No way. I don't think he has murder in him. Sometimes you know what people are capable of and what they're not. He might have wanted to get away from her at the end, but he'd never do something like this."

"But who, then?"

He paused, placing his hands on his hips. "I don't know. I ask myself that every night. That poor little baby never had a chance."

The words sank in so slowly, Kelsey actually felt the weight of them pressing her closer to the ground. All this time they'd been talking about Becca Cooper he never let it slip that he knew she was pregnant. Not once. "You knew about that?" It didn't seem possible. Maybe she'd heard wrong.

"Course I did. You even put it in the newspaper story. Heck, if it'd happened sooner, I might have been the father." He must have noticed her mouth had collapsed into a pout. "I've disappointed you, haven't I?"

"Of course not," she lied. "You're a big boy. Whatever happened between you and Becca is none of my business." If he believed that, he'd believe anything.

"C'mon Kelsey, I've let you down." He reached for her hand and squeezed it tightly. "You need to know I'm no saint. I've never pretended to be one, either."

Before she could say more, a figure appeared on the horizon in front of them. Sergeant Hines had come a different way up the bayou. To tell the truth, she was thankful for the diversion. She was beginning to feel foolish, though she didn't quite know why. "He's here."

Nothing stirred in the stillness; even the cicadas were sleeping. The figure grew larger and larger, until finally Sergeant Hines walked up to them. He wasn't wearing his uniform today, but a pair of well-worn jeans and a plaid work shirt. He looked younger out of the uniform and more relaxed, as if starch had held everything in before and now he could finally breathe.

"Hello, again. Interesting place to meet up."

"I wanted to see the place where Becca died."

The sergeant placed his hands on his hips, just like Park. It seemed to be a natural stance for him. "We've gone over this scene a half-dozen times and didn't find more than flat grass and mud tracks. Can't see it'll do much good to repeat ourselves."

"Sometimes you never realize what's missing until you find it, right?" She hadn't meant to sound like a fortune in a cookie, but at the moment they didn't have much to go on and the stakes had risen. "Can't we look once more?"

The two men glanced at each other. Something transpired in the silence, because Park spoke next. "Of course we can. Isn't that right, Uncle George?"

"Suit yourself." The sergeant pointed to the barricade behind them. "Why don't we start over there? We took everything inside the tape, so maybe we should search the perimeter."

Together, they turned. The air above the ground shimmered as heat rose from the dust. In front of them, brittle afternoon sun glanced sharply off the pin oaks. The plastic caution tape, once stretched taut across the sawhorses, now sagged in the middle, limp and lifeless.

Sergeant Hines paused by the site. "Almost forgot to tell you. You can cross one more suspect off our list."

Kelsey followed his eyes to the crime scene. Aside from Lilli-Fay Holiday, who spent the morning of Becca's murder on the telephone with a home shopping show, no one else had been cleared. "Do tell."

"Ran a check on Velma Wainwright this morning."

Reverend Holiday's assistant. The woman who loathed Becca

Cooper for her part in her affair with Bobby Holiday, from what Kelsey could tell. That morning in the sanctuary, Velma had all but admitted taking pleasure from Becca's murder.

"Turns out she plays bingo every Friday down at the veteran's lodge. Has since 1960." Sergeant Hines chuckled. "Guess winning fifty dollars is a big deal, because everyone remembers Velma cashing in that morning."

Kelsey knew the place. A squat building with a tin roof on one of the many farm roads that bisected Enterprise. How many times had she driven by the property, where a homemade sign advertised weekly bingo games hosted by the grand and benevolent order of the lodge? "Are you sure? She sounded awfully mad at Becca Cooper when I went to church last Sunday. She pretty much said she was glad Becca had died."

"I've got a sworn statement from the exalted leader himself. Velma took home fifty dollars and change on a Texas-T card. Couldn't make up that kind of detail. I'd say she's out of the running."

Park nodded after listening to his uncle. "They take bingo pretty seriously over there. If they said Velma Wainwright took home the pot, she took home the pot."

Silence fell over the group, each of its members lost in thought. The list of suspects had dwindled again. Chief among them was Bobby Holiday, but there was also the violent ex-husband, and even the Goth teenager who had found her body. And, Park, of course. He seemed to know Becca better than most of the others.

"Let's go over there." Best to change the subject before anyone gave voice to her fears. Kelsey wandered closer to the bayou, to a stand of reeds standing stick-straight in the heavy air. She poked at them haphazardly with her foot.

"We've already looked at the blood-stain pattern," the sergeant told her. "There was some blood matted in her hair, plus the drip stains and the cast-off stains, so we know she was murdered on the scene." As a former homicide detective, Sergeant Hines must have seen hundreds of crime scenes, and the horror had long ago worn off. "She'd been hit right here on the bayou, since there was a cast-off pattern to the stain. There were several stains, each a couple millimeters."

"You've searched the rest of the bayou, I suppose?" Park was one step ahead of her apparently, because he seemed to know exactly what to look for. She had no idea. She hoped something would magically appear, but such a miracle didn't seem too likely.

"Of course. Nothing. Won't have the coroner's report for a few days, though."

Kelsey listened intently while she ran her foot through the tall reeds. She finally gave up, and turned to rejoin the men on the path, when something caught her eye. "What's this?" She bent lower to take a look, noticing a clear imprint next to a clump of reeds. A zigzag imprint. A capital "N", plain as day. "Look at this." She motioned for Sergeant Hines and Park to join her on her perch. "What's it mean?"

Both men immediately walked to her side, Park squatting on his haunches to see whatever it was she was talking about. "I'd say something heavy hit right there. Look, it smashed the reeds next to it in a perfect line."

"Could be nothing," Sergeant Hines said. "Maybe a toad left it, maybe a bird's egg." Quickly, he withdrew a disposable camera from the pocket of his shirt. After forwarding the film, he leaned closer and took several pictures of the imprint.

"Something had to be awfully heavy to leave such a clean outline." Kelsey squinted at the ground. "I mean, look at it. It looks like someone stamped a perfect N in the dirt. How often does that happen?"

Sergeant Hines shook his head. "Like I said, don't get too

worked up, but we'll see what the lab says. Does look mighty intentional, though."

"Not too far from where she lay, wouldn't you say?" Park pointed to the site of the smashed reeds with the track marks.

The group stared at the ground for several more minutes. One by one, they straightened. "Something fell right there, something heavy," Kelsey said. It felt good to be useful. Renewed by her discovery, she took several more steps closer to the water, until the thought of river rats stopped her short. "May I have some help here?"

Park eyed his uncle briefly before joining her on the slope and offering her his hand.

"You two seem mighty comfortable with each other. Why don't you kids keep looking around here, and I'll see what's on the other side of the path." He turned away from them, and quickly sidestepped up the incline to the walking path above.

"That was subtle." Kelsey shook her head and took another step closer to the bayou. Together, she and Park combed the area for several minutes, finding nothing. When they had finished their search, they turned to leave.

"If this bayou could talk, I wonder what it'd say." Kelsey posed the question to no one in particular, and she didn't expect an answer.

"I think it'd say things happen here that you want no part of. Have you seen enough?"

The truth was, she was starting to tire of the hot sun and still air. "I guess. At least Becca's murder seems more real now. I always wondered where they found her body."

"Now you know. Come on, let's get out of here."

They walked up the incline and rejoined Sergeant Hines on the path. After spending an hour in the dry, dusty elements, Kelsey was relieved to be leaving the scene.

"I'll get this film to the lab." Sergeant Hines patted his shirt pocket. "Have 'em blow it up for us. Why don't you two check back with me tonight or tomorrow, and we'll go over what we've got."

Kelsey glanced at Park. "Guess that means we have some time to kill."

"Interesting choice of words." Park squinted toward the west, into the waning sun. "I know a way we could fill that time." The skin puckered at his eyes when he drew his brows together like that. "Yep, I know just the thing."

They said good-bye to Sergeant Hines and walked toward Park's pickup. Kelsey was too exhausted to even question his response. The threatening phone call that morning, trolling the bayou for clues in Becca's murder, not to mention the ongoing tension of not knowing what would happen on any given day, had started to take their toll on her. Much as she hated to admit it, a good, long nap sounded like the best idea.

"Hop up. I've got something that'll take your mind off all this."

He drove them back onto the highway, where they headed west until the telephone wires gradually thinned and the few billboards that were there ended altogether. The road meandered through fields of rice, recently turned, with red dirt capping the crests of soil. Even though Park had blasted the air conditioning to "high," Kelsey rolled down the window to let a breeze whip through the cab. An earthy smell of moist roots, indistinguishable bulbs, and cattle filled the pickup. She laid her head against the leather seat and sighed.

"You okay?"

When she turned to face Park, she saw a tin structure in the distance, its roof glinting in the late afternoon sun. "Fine. Just fine."

They turned onto a gravel road a few yards farther down, where a wooden sign announced the location of "Flying D Aviation." The pickup rattled along the gravel path until they pulled up to the metal structure, its roll gate lifted to expose a pair of aircraft inside. The cavernous space also held some rusted drums, a tower of tools, several ladders, and a pile of rolled-up banners in the corner.

Kelsey cocked her head and waited as Park jumped from the cab and circled around to her door. He swept it open and motioned toward the hangar. "Ever been up in a prop plane before?"

"You're kidding." She hopped onto pea gravel, which crunched under her feet. Thank goodness she'd worn flats again. That was another credo she lived by as a reporter: never wear shoes too high to run in. She never knew what factory, or warehouse—or airplane hangar, for that matter—she might end up in.

She tiptoed to the nearest plane. Sunshine yellow with a blue racing stripe and checkerboard on its tail, it reminded her of a child's toy. All that had been added was a pipe that ran under the cockpit, from wingtip to wingtip, probably fifty feet in all. She guessed that was where Park released his chemicals and water and what-not onto the land below. The cockpit windows were open, and behind the pilot's red seat she saw a smaller seat tucked into the back. Evidently that was her seat. Though she had no idea how she was going to reach it, since the cockpit towered nearly ten feet in the air.

"You look worried." Park stood next to her.

She shrugged, as if she spent every day next to a half-million-dollar toy that would soon lift her into the sky.

"Don't worry. I'll help you up." Before he climbed onto the wing, though, Park circled the plane and began to perform what she assumed was the pre-flight checkup. He tinkered with several mechanisms, while she wandered to the back of the hangar. She knew that as an ag pilot he sprayed crops for bugs and diseases for a living, and he explained during their date the night before he even helped oil companies clean up after their spills. Said he dropped something called "disintegrators" right onto the oil slicks and they would magically disappear.

"Almost done," he called out to her, his head bent over an open flap on the side of the plane.

"Take your time." She made it a point never to rush a professional, especially one who would soon have her soaring a thousand feet into the air. "I can wait."

"All done." He slammed a flap down and patted the side of the plane. "This one's my favorite. I call her *Tejas.*"

She crinkled her nose. "Why that?"

"These planes are built right here in Texas," he said proudly.

"You act like it's your child."

"Costs about the same. If it wasn't for the oil field jobs there's no way I could afford her." He took Kelsey by the elbow and guided her to the wing. "Step right here. Don't worry, you won't break anything."

Not quite convinced, Kelsey stepped onto the wing, then hoisted herself into the cockpit. She had to step over the pilot's seat to do that, and noticed the instrument panel with its gizmos, gadgets, and numbers. "You sure you don't want to check everything one more time?"

He laughed. "We're good. Just grab one of those helmets and hold on tight."

She did as she was told and watched him also climb into the cockpit, easing his large frame into the cramped space. Unlike her, he seemed perfectly at home amid the controls and contraptions. He put on a helmet, too, but his had a microphone built into it that fit below his chin. In a moment, she heard a crackle in her ear as his voice sounded inside her helmet.

"Now don't worry about a thing. I've been doing this since I was a teenager."

She wanted to give him some smart-alecky response, but realized her helmet didn't come equipped with a microphone. How convenient. That way he couldn't hear her scream her lungs out. He turned around and gave her the "thumbs up" sign before easing the plane out of the hangar and onto the gravel drive.

She squeezed her eyes shut. What had possessed her to agree to this? She should have been back at home, snuggled under the covers of her bed, not waiting to take off in a tin can, albeit a very sophisticated tin can.

A moment later, he guided the airplane onto a cement landing strip he'd built out back of the hangar. Within seconds, the dull sound of the engine crescendoed to a high-pitched whine. She kept her eyes shut as the plane lifted off the ground, suddenly weightless. Unlike a commercial plane, though, where the sensation was numbed by layers of steel and luggage, here she felt every switch and sway as the plane fought to rise higher and higher in the sky.

By the time she opened her eyes, they were soaring above Enterprise, into the sun. Thanks to the tinting on the helmet's visor, she could see past the glare to the aqua sky, the emerald trees, the chocolate brown fields. At a thousand feet, every color seemed sharp, as if she could reach out and poke the sky and her fingers would leave a smudge.

She tapped Park's shoulder to get his attention.

"What do you think? Pretty cool, isn't it?" he said into her ear.

Even though he couldn't see her, she nodded her head, so entranced with the view that she forgot to feel afraid. He flew them for a while longer, then guided the plane into a smooth turn, pointing them back toward town. She'd never been so thrilled with anything in her life. So this was why people had such a fascination with airplanes. She could understand the love affair, now. It was the closest she'd ever get to soaring, to knowing what an eagle or a hawk or even a tiny sparrow must feel like.

The earth shrank even more as Park piloted them higher in the sky. From their vantage spot, she could make out the white steeple of Second Coming—Reverend Holiday's church—which looked like a piece on a game board made of molded plastic. Look . . . there was the Enterprise Police Department, with all that land around it, a cement block in a sea of asphalt. It didn't take long for them to finish their tour of Enterprise, and Kelsey hoped he'd circle back again to give her another view of the town. Funny how clear and clean and perfect everything looked from this distance, as if not one thing were out of place on the diorama below. No trash, no graffiti, no rusted-out cars could ever be glimpsed from this height.

She was about to tap him on the shoulder again, to signal that he should point them back toward the hangar, when he suddenly dipped the wing dramatically to the right. Her stomach lurched as nausea washed over her. Something foul-tasting filled her mouth and throat; something that burned.

She slapped the back of his helmet, but he only laughed into the microphone. Instead of righting the aircraft, he flew them at that sickening angle for a second or two longer. Frantically, she hit his helmet again. She didn't want to throw up into her own helmet, but if she stayed at that angle one . . . more . . . minute, that's exactly what would happen.

Once again, he laughed. Didn't he understand that she was serious? Didn't he care?

Finally, after an eternity, he righted the aircraft and the horizon leveled off. Maybe he had a cruel streak in him, after all. She kept her eyes trained on the roll of leather at the base of his helmet because she could no longer stomach seeing the ground rush by beneath them.

In a few minutes they'd be back on land again; the beautiful, hard-packed pea gravel. She couldn't wait to return to the hangar and feel stones crunch beneath her flats. Then she'd give him a piece of her mind. Could it be the picture-perfect man she'd dreamt about all night long had a dark side she hadn't noticed before? What other things didn't she know about Park Daniels?

CHAPTER 13

The knock on the door took LilliFay by surprise. She glanced through the peephole to see Velma, of all people, standing on the stoop. Not once in the last thirty years had that woman paid a formal visit to the house, other than the occasional Christmas party or New Year's get-together. Oh, she might nod at her in church or compliment LilliFay on one of her hats if she was feeling charitable, but to drive to the house and appear on Lilli-Fay's doorstep? That took extra effort. Whatever could Velma want on the tail end of this Wednesday afternoon?

LilliFay pulled the chain back on the lock and opened the door. Sure enough, Velma didn't look exactly comfortable standing there in the hot sun like an egg in a frying pan. She'd probably be more comfortable if LilliFay invited her into the foyer.

"Come on inside. You're going to fry out there."

"Don't mind if I do." Stiffly, Velma walked into the foyer. She wore a simple shift and had twisted her hair into a bun, like always. It aged her terribly, but LilliFay didn't feel comfortable offering her fashion advice, since Velma had worn her hair like that all her life and probably would until the day she died. The good news was that LilliFay never had to worry about Velma trying to steal her man. Now Becca Cooper . . . that was another story.

Velma followed her through the shadowy hall, into the living room. It was too early for supper and not quite the right time for a cup of tea. The awkward hour between five and six o'clock, which put her at a loss for what to do. Most days she flicked on the home shopping channel and let it drone on and on as she picked up the kitchen. She did like to have the kitchen picked up before Bobby got home.

"Have a seat." She pointed to the kitchen table, and took a chair opposite Velma. Luckily, she'd already wiped the table clean, or she'd have been mortified to have Velma stare at it like that. "Would you like some water?" No telling what else she had to offer in the refrigerator. It wasn't as if the visit had been planned or anything. If it had, she might have properly prepared some lemonade or iced tea.

"No, thank you." With her sitting there all proper, it was hard for LilliFay to read Velma. She obviously had a point to make, but she was taking her sweet time getting there. "I hope I'm not bothering you, LilliFay."

"Bothering me?" Now why would Velma think that? Even though they hadn't been friends for lo, these many years, they hadn't exactly been enemies, either. No, they were more like long-standing acquaintances who happened to go to the same church and happened to spend time with the same man.

"Bobby's still at the church, if that's who you've come to see." Though heaven only knew there would be little enough for him to do there, now. Maybe wrap up a few counseling sessions, call a few of his favorite parishioners, write a few notes for the next pastor in line. Things were winding down, coming to a close. It felt like a formality now for him to visit the church, he'd said.

"No, I actually came to see you." Velma glanced around the kitchen sheepishly. "I see you've kept things about the same. Can't believe I haven't been here since that Christmas party back in 'ninety-nine."

"Has it been that long?" Amazing how quickly time had flown. Why, it seemed like yesterday Bobby had introduced her to his secretary, probably hoping they'd become fast friends. "I've changed the curtains out. Used to be yellow gingham, but Bobby didn't much care for them." LilliFay pointed to the material hanging over the kitchen sink. "The check's new."

"So it is." Velma leaned forward, still empty-handed.

"Can I at least get you some ice water, Velma? Doesn't feel right to have you sit in my kitchen with nothing to drink."

"Okay. That would be nice."

LilliFay rose and opened a kitchen cabinet. She pulled out a glass and walked to the refrigerator to fill it with ice cubes. Once she placed the glass under the water dispenser, liquid rose to the top in a swirl of bubbles.

"Remember that Christmas party with all the deacons?" Velma asked.

"The one where Ted Junior got drunk and ended up in my rosebushes?" LilliFay chuckled. She walked back to the table and set the glass in front of Velma.

"The very same. I don't think Bobby ever figured out how one of his deacons smuggled a flask through the front door."

"Never imagined he hid it in his sock. That was a good party, all right." A house full of people singing Christmas carols and every once in a while ducking out back to have a nip. If Bobby had only known.

"Think he ever figured it out?" Velma reached for the glass.

"Nah. Bobby always thinks the best of everyone. Probably thought Ted Junior was being silly. Course, he went head first into the bark mulch."

The women burst out laughing. What a night. Oh, but a lot of Christmases had come and gone since then. Some good, some bad, but always, there was the church. "He's going to miss it, Velma."

Velma took a long drink of water before speaking. When she lowered the glass, her eyes looked somber. "A lot of people are talking. Saying that maybe Bobby was behind all this with Becca."

LilliFay nodded. "I know. Even though they don't say anything to me, they usually hush up when I come around." It had gotten so bad, she purposefully visited the market first thing in the morning, when most people were still in bed. That way they wouldn't see her in the frozen food section and look away. "It's gotten awkward, that's for sure."

Velma traced a pattern on the fogged glass. Around and around, as she watched the pattern form.

"Why are you here, Velma? Do you want to talk about Bobby? Is that it?"

It was so hard to read her face. Troubled, surely, but also hesitant. "You could say that."

"Out with it, Velma. What's going on?" The world could crash around them, and Velma would sit there with her lips pursed, her face a blank canvas. "We don't have all day. Unless you want to stay for dinner?" Maybe it *would* be nice to finally have another person at the dinner table. Not that she was sick of Bobby or anything, but with a lot more time on his hands, she imagined they'd spend hundreds of dinners together in the years to come.

"Okay, okay." Velma seemed to marshal her strength, because she tucked her shoulders back. "I want you to know about something. It happened a week back, in the choir room." Velma fell quiet, as if she needed to organize her thoughts again. "No, it was before then. I don't usually go in there, of course. It's not my place. No need for me to poke through things in the choir loft."

LilliFay leaned forward, even though they were all alone in the kitchen.

"Anyway, I went back to see if maybe the bulletins got delivered there by accident. Harvey's our normal delivery man, but he took sick that week, so it was someone new. Couldn't find the bulletins to save my life."

"Go on, Velma." Honestly, they'd both grow old waiting for her to get to the point.

"Well." Velma reached again for the glass of water.

Now LilliFay regretted putting a prop in Velma's hands because the story would take twice as long to finish. She reached out and grasped Velma's hand so she couldn't grip the drink. "Okay, so you were in the choir room. What happened?"

Velma gulped, but she left her hand under LilliFay's. "Wouldn't you know it, two people were already in there, and they were arguing. It was ugly."

"Who was it?"

"That's the thing. I could only see one of them. It was *her.*"

"You mean Becca?" Almost touching how Velma couldn't bring herself to say Becca's name. As if speaking it would dirty LilliFay's kitchen. "You can say her name. I don't mind."

"No. As long as I'm alive, I'll never say her name again." Velma looked determined now. Whatever else might be said about Velma Wainwright, she was nothing if not loyal. To Bobby, to the church, and apparently, even to LilliFay.

"Anyway . . . you were saying?" A cuckoo clock in the living room kept time for them with a gentle beat. Even if Velma wasn't going to stay for supper, LilliFay would need to fix Bobby's food soon. She didn't have all the time in the world.

"Well, they were arguing about something. That woman was all red in the face, she was yelling so hard. And I could see someone's back, and he was wearing a starched white shirt, but I didn't recognize him." Velma finally withdrew her hand and laid it in her lap. "I've never heard such words as what she said to him. Mercy . . . it wasn't fit for polite company."

"Did you know who it was? Could you tell by his voice?" The story had taken a while to make sense, but now the pieces had begun to click into place. Somewhere was a man who had argued with Becca before her death, and that man obviously wasn't her Bobby.

"No, darn it. He was going to speak, but then the delivery-man came up behind me and nearly scared me to death. He picked a fine time to finally show up with the bulletins."

LilliFay reached across the table, and, without thinking, took a slow drink of Velma's water. Not a polite move, but Velma wouldn't mind, what with the dramatics taking place. "That's mighty interesting, Velma. You said that happened about a week ago?"

"Yep. Thursday night. Do you think we should tell Bobby?"

"Oh, no." Bobby had enough to think about; there was no use to drag him into this. Plus, there wasn't a blessed thing he could do with the information. "We have to go tell Sergeant Hines. He's the one needs to know."

"I suppose you're right. But do you think we could keep my name out of this?"

"No promises, but I think you've done your job by telling me. He'll be mighty interested in that story."

Stepping out of the airplane, back at the landing strip, Kelsey wobbled onto the concrete and ripped the helmet from her head.

"Park! How could you do that to me? I was terrified."

He looked genuinely surprised. "I wanted to show you a few tricks. I thought it'd be fun up there."

She clenched her teeth and shoved the helmet at him. "You thought wrong." Her stomach still felt queasy as she made her way back to the hangar, relieved to be on terra firma again.

"Kelsey . . . I'm sorry." Park rushed to catch up with her, then cradled the helmet in his other arm while he gripped her elbow. "Don't be mad. I was just having a little fun up there. I won't do it again."

"You're right, buster, because there won't be another time." She jerked her arm away from his hand and stomped back to the waiting doors of the airplane hangar. She refused to turn around and look at him, because she knew if she did, those eyes of his would melt her on the spot.

He'd landed them safely, after all. And he did apologize. That didn't give him the right to play daredevil with her in the backseat, though. "Look, can you just take me back home, please? I want to get my car and go to the newsroom."

She could only imagine how Renee was faring back at the *Caller,* trying to do both their jobs while she'd been up in the air with Park, losing her lunch. Not that the paper was as busy as the Los Angeles newspaper or anything, but people did call about ad rates, or send press releases for special events, or drop by with copy for wedding announcements. No telling what could have happened even in the short time she'd been out flying with Park. "I feel guilty about Renee being there all by herself."

Park looked doubtful. "You sure? What if that guy calls the newsroom again?"

No, she wasn't sure, but it didn't feel right to bail on Renee, either. Plus, she needed a little time to let her stomach settle and her anger thaw. "He probably won't call twice in one day." She even faked a smile for Park's benefit. "I'll let you know if he does, and you can hunt him down with your Remington."

"Don't mess with me, Kelsey. I just might." Park seemed at ease at the idea of protecting her with a shotgun. Such a different country she'd landed in when she moved to Enterprise. "Tell you what." He ran his hand along her arm. "What if I stop by later and keep you company?"

The nerves on her skin tingled under his touch. *Damn it.* "Maybe. I don't know. Okay, I guess so." She hated herself for being such an easy mark. But he did seem sorry about the crazy plane ride, after all. "I should be home around eight or so."

"Done." With a gentle touch, he retraced the path of his hand. "I'll even bring over the beer this time."

What was it about this man that made her knees feel like buckling, even when he had just toyed with her nerves? She walked with him back to the pickup, more confused than ever. They drove in silence until they reached her street, and he dropped her off in front of the cottage. A flash of smile, a wave of the hand, and he was gone. She sighed, pulled out her car keys, and fired up her car before she could change her mind.

Just as she had thought, by the time she pulled into the parking lot of the newsroom, several cars were already there. Another pickup, plus a vintage sedan and a dusty SUV. Renee immediately brightened when Kelsey walked into the room. Three people stood at the counter, all filling out forms, and all with checks in their hands.

"I thought I told you to take some time off." Renee tried to sound angry, but couldn't pull it off.

"Missed you, too." Kelsey smiled at her and swung open the barroom-type gate that separated the lobby from the newsroom in the back. "See? You need me." She dropped her purse to the floor and stepped up to the counter.

"We've got two classifieds and a display ad. Can you please get this man a rate card?"

Kelsey reached under the counter and withdrew a laminated card that gave column inches and dollar amounts. "What size?" Back in journalism school, which seemed like a hundred years ago now, no one ever told her she'd be doing advertising sales along with writing copy, interviewing people, and taking her own pictures sometimes. Newspapers were a business, after all, and what with the Internet biting into their sales, they needed every print ad they could get. It was all hands on deck at times like this.

"Half-page."

Next to her, Renee accepted a check from one of their customers and handed the woman an advertising packet in return. "If you want more business at the drugstore, you should think about running a bigger ad," she told the stranger, who tucked the packet under her arm and left the newsroom. "Oh, I almost forgot." Renee turned her attention to the next person in line as she spoke. "You've got some messages on your desk. For some reason a Dallas news editor called you. Twice. Sounded important."

Kelsey frowned. The Dallas paper? Since when did they call such a small newsroom as hers? She placed a rate card on the counter. Maybe they wanted to use one of the freelancers, or hire out a sports photographer. Kelsey left the customer with the rate card and ducked back to her desk and a pile of ice-blue telephone messages. Sure enough, two of them held the name and phone number for the city editor at the Dallas newspaper.

She glanced at the counter where a decision must have been made, because the customer withdrew his checkbook. She returned to the counter to find he'd picked a four-color ad to run Saturday, their highest-circulation day. *Jackpot.* It didn't get any better than a four-color weekend ad. She accepted his check and wandered back to the telephone, leaving Renee with the lone customer in the newsroom. Quickly, she dialed the number for the Dallas paper before anyone else could wander through the front door.

"City desk." The voice, flat and brusque, could have belonged to any editor at any newspaper.

"Hi. I'm returning a phone call from Jason Lee. This is Kelsey Garrett from the *Enterprise Country Caller.*" She winced as soon as the words left her mouth. Usually, when someone asked her the name of the paper she shortened it to *Enterprise Caller* so they wouldn't get the image of a backwater newspaper printed on a homemade press. Maybe the name "Country Caller" sounded decent a century ago, but it seemed silly now.

There was some static on the other end and a voice called out, "Jason! Line two." Just enough time to catch her breath before someone new came on the line.

"Jason Lee." No greeting. No warmth. Just the facts, ma'am.

"Hi, Mr. Lee. You called me earlier. This is Kelsey Garrett with the paper in Enterprise." She wasn't going to make the same mistake twice.

"Oh, yeah. It's the *Country Caller* right?" He sounded amused. Or maybe it was only her imagination as she pictured him smirking into the telephone.

"The very same. How may I help you?" While he had yet to exchange any pleasantries, it never hurt to be polite.

"Saw your byline today. Good job on the piece about the murder investigation."

Time slowed as Kelsey pressed the receiver against her ear.

"We're short here by two reporters. Lost 'em both to corporate jobs. How about you send me your portfolio so I can see what you've done."

"My portfolio?" As if the man had spoken another language and she needed to translate his remarks. "Of course. No problem. I'll email you some clips."

"Good. Show me some features, some hard news. You know, mix it up. My email's on the website."

She gathered her thoughts enough at last to thank him for his request, but the line went dead before she could speak. These guys didn't mess around. The story had only appeared on the wire report that morning, and already she had a request for writing samples. She glanced up to see Renee watching her from across the room.

"What's up?" Renee stood all alone at the counter, the last customer gone. Peace and quiet had returned to the newsroom, and the comforting drone of the printing press next door hummed through the wall.

"Hmmm." Kelsey shrugged, certain Renee could read her thoughts even from ten feet away. "No big deal. Did you get my copy this morning?"

Renee cocked her head. "Yep. Looked good. I sent you back the edits." She still looked doubtful, but didn't ask her anything more about the telephone call.

Thank goodness Kelsey had decided to return to the newsroom. She had everything she needed to fill Jason Lee's request. Somehow, the atmosphere in the newsroom seemed lighter, brighter, now. He'd asked for the clips right away. Which meant he was serious about hiring someone. And she had as much chance as anyone else. . . .

Kelsey hummed as she clicked on her terminal. She had more than enough material to send him. The edits from Renee would have to wait a little longer as she sent her work in to one of the biggest newspapers in all of Texas.

Of course, Dallas was four hours north of Houston. A long commute from Enterprise by anyone's standards. What would people think if they knew she was applying for the job? It was too early in her relationship with Park to have to think about that, wasn't it? Plus, he'd made her so mad that afternoon. The Dallas paper was one of the biggest newspapers in the country, for goodness sake. She continued to type.

"You're busy over there." Renee had returned to her desk, and peered at her from behind a computer monitor.

"Me? Just doing my job." She settled back into the chair as the monitor came alive. Amazing how quickly things could turn around, when one least expected it.

By the time Kelsey flicked off the monitor, the sky outside the newsroom's window had darkened. She rolled her stiff shoulders forward and switched off the computer. *What a day.* The muscles in her neck and back ached from the hours she'd spent hunched over the computer. Between finding the right clips to send to the editor in Dallas, to rewriting her copy for Renee, she hadn't stretched but once or twice in at least an hour.

She straightened, a little at a time, all alone in the newsroom. Renee had finally called it quits around seven, and the sports reporter spent his nights at the ball field this time of year. The men who ran the printing press next door were long gone, since they normally pulled in before sunup. No matter. Truth be told, she liked the silence and coziness of knowing she had the whole newsroom to herself. As if she were the master of her own little universe, keeping watch over Enterprise while the rest of the town relaxed.

She switched off the overheads before dead-bolting the newsroom door. Warmth radiated from the asphalt through the soles of her shoes when she walked outside, a reminder of the hot afternoon sun. Nights like this made her thankful she lived away from the city because a million stars twinkled overhead, protecting her as she drove down Fifth Street.

Amazing how quickly things could change. She'd gone from a terrible threat that morning to a sweltering afternoon on the bayou viewing a crime scene, to a crazy airplane ride with Park. But now, under a canopy of pin lights, she felt content as she drove through the city square.

Lights glowed from homes to her right and left, and occasionally the blue flicker of a television spilled onto a lawn. By now soccer practices and tap-dance lessons had ended, giving way to family suppers and homework. Normally, she might feel a little melancholy seeing such domestic scenes. Not tonight. Tonight she'd have her own company coming to visit her in about an hour. She pulled onto her street, only vaguely aware of a glow somewhere behind her car.

The glow grew nearer and nearer as she drove along her street. Amazing how every detail stood out at twenty miles an hour. A chunk of curb was still missing at the corner, a gaping V-cut that looked like it had been purposefully carved. A bicycle lay sideways in a nearby driveway, its pedals tinged with rust. Finally, she couldn't take it anymore and decided to pull over and let the impatient driver behind her pass.

She reached for the blinker, when something slammed into the back of her car so hard she jerked forward, stopping a hairsbreadth from the wheel. The seatbelt bit into her shoulder and she heard the screech of metal hitting metal. The driver behind her hadn't slowed, after all. He'd gunned the engine and slammed into the back of her car.

She glanced into the rearview mirror, where a blinding flash of high beams made her look away. Was the driver behind her drunk? Stupid? She slowed even more, prepared to turn into the next driveway and confront him or her. God only knew what was waiting for her when she stopped the car and went back to inspect her bumper. If he thought he was going to drive away without giving her an insurance card—

She turned the wheel right, but the lights behind her sped up yet again, and she felt the shoulder strap bite into her skin once more as the car behind her slammed into her bumper. This time her car lurched right and clipped a metal mailbox. The side mirror flew off, disappearing into the night sky. This was for real. This was on purpose. Nothing made sense as she jammed on the brakes and plowed through a row of scraggly bushes.

A deep survival instinct surfaced inside her. She had to get away. Now. She threw the steering wheel hard to the left, and her car skidded onto a driveway. The car fishtailed, and the right side slammed into someone's garage door. Frantically, she hit the gas, but the car sputtered forward and careened into a basketball hoop, the hood of the car crumbling under the impact.

Then . . . mercifully . . . silence. A porch light flickered on as she laid her forehead against the steering wheel, her head throbbing against the cool plastic.

"What the—" A second later, the owner of the voice appeared at her window. "Are you all right?"

The door opened, she slumped forward, and the stranger reached for her shoulders. Her fingers still gripped the steering wheel so tightly, she could feel cold steel under the vinyl cover.

Slowly, she turned her head toward the sound of the voice. An old man stared at her, his eyes wide with surprise. "Call the police," she mumbled, forcing the words from her throat. "The police," she repeated. Finally, her fingers slipped from the steering wheel and her head fell against the vinyl upholstery.

CHAPTER 14

The road to Park Daniels' airplane hangar curved through freshly tilled fields of rice. By fall the stalks would brush his kneecap, Bobby knew, but for now it was red dirt as far as the eye could see.

He guided his sedan through another curve. Ahead, the tin roof of the airplane hangar appeared on the horizon. Shards of pink and red shot from the metal outbuilding like sparks lit by the setting sun. Between fertilizing local crops, keeping the bugs off them, and cleaning up oil spills in the Gulf of Mexico, Park had built himself quite a little business on the outskirts of Enterprise, all right.

Bobby drove all the way to the end of the drive, where a freshly painted wooden sign announced "Flying D Aviation." He pulled up alongside the hangar and parked the car. He'd miss this once he moved from Enterprise. Land rippling to the end of the horizon, stretching for miles in every direction. Soil underneath his feet instead of hard tile, like at the church. One of the last few places on God's green where a man could stop and think, unencumbered by noise and deadlines and crowds. Where silence filled you so full, the sound of a cow lowing might come as a great surprise.

He swung open his door and stepped onto clay earth and pea gravel. Both of Park's airplanes were tethered down. One, a bright yellow model, had its engine flap peeled back to expose glinting metal inside. Park—standing on the last step of an extension ladder—leaned over the engine with a crescent wrench in one hand and an oily rag in the other.

"Hello," Bobby called out. He approached cautiously, thankful he'd had the good sense to remove his suit jacket before he'd left the church. This was no place for two-piece suits or freshly shined wingtips. What he'd come to ask would make him feel awkward enough without the extra stiffness that came from wearing a business suit.

"Evening, Reverend." Park laid the crescent wrench down and nodded in greeting. The airplane glowed in the dusky light. Bobby knew that it was one of the best models available.

He recalled how Park had once said that new farming methods nearly destroyed the whole field of agricultural flying some years back. Now that farmers could grow twice the crops on half the land, they didn't much need the fertilizers and insecticides, the seeds and herbicides that agricultural pilots had to offer. So the successful ones, like Park, learned to hire out to oil companies to clean up the messes left by broken tanker ships in the Gulf. Flew low over the waves and dropped disintegrators right onto the gooey blobs, so Park had told him.

"Your plane's looking good, Park." Had to hand it to him, all right. Maybe they weren't so different after all. While Bobby spent his time spreading the Lord's word over Enterprise, the Flying D spread out chemicals to clean up and protect the earth.

"What can I do for you?" Park leaned against the plane, a bicep bulging under his white t-shirt. It wasn't hard to see why Becca Cooper had taken a liking to him. All the girls seemed to like Park Daniels.

"Wanted to chat a bit." Even though a light breeze blew through the hangar, Bobby felt his face and neck warm. He loosened the knot on his tie, which didn't help much. "Could you come down? Please."

Park shot him a curious look, then began to descend the ladder. So warm here in the hangar. Bobby pulled at the knot on his neck again, hoping to cool down some. "I thought it was about time we had a talk. About Becca."

The two stood eye to eye now. Park probably sensed the gravity of the situation, because he crossed his arms in front of his chest and, thankfully, remained silent.

"I need to ask you something." Bobby glanced around the hangar, searching for somewhere, anywhere, to sit. Ever since he began preaching at Second Coming, he felt more comfortable with a barrier –like a podium—in front of him. Take away that barrier and he felt vulnerable, naked, as if the other person could read his mind. His eyes rested on a few barrels of oil sitting in the corner, which were just the right height for perching. "Do you mind?" He nodded toward the barrels.

Once they had settled on top of the barrels, Park finally relaxed his arms. "Are you going to tell me what this is about, Reverend, or do I have to guess?"

My, but he looked like his uncle when he stared at him like that. Right after they'd found Becca's body, the sergeant had come to the church and asked Bobby question after question, an hour's worth in all. The two had known each other for decades, which made the questions even more painful than if they'd been strangers to each other. How often had he and Becca used the condo? Is that where they always met up? And just what was he thinking, cheating on LilliFay like that? It was a dark hour indeed, his shame laid bare. He began to sob at one point during the interview with the police sergeant, which seemed to mortify George more than anything else, because he studied his hands as if he'd never seen them before.

Bobby hadn't meant to confess his sins like that. Standing there in the half-light with Park, memories of that afternoon washed over him, and Bobby's eyes welled up all over again.

Park and Becca. Now that had made sense. If only he'd been man enough to walk away, instead of running to her and her lemon perfume. "It's time for me to ask you something, Park."

"Go on, then."

After all that had happened, Park never seemed to blame Bobby, which amazed him no end. After all, Park could have stayed with Becca, if only Bobby hadn't gotten in the way. She told Bobby later that Park left her when he found out about their affair. She told him that one night when they met up at the condo, and his respect for Park grew ten-fold.

But now . . . now with Becca's murder, everything had changed. His own priorities had changed. "You knew Becca was going to have a baby, right?" He continued, without waiting for an answer. "Was it yours?" Bobby watched Park carefully, watched for some sign of what the young man might be thinking. He felt he owed it to Becca and the unborn child to set the record straight. The truth wouldn't make it all better—it never could—but at least the child would have a father in the end. He owed Becca that much. They all did.

"No. It wasn't." Park uncrossed his arms. "I broke it off a long time ago. Couldn't go out with her when I knew you were seeing her, too."

Sitting there on the barrels, watching the setting sun, Bobby studied Park for the longest time. No doubt about it—the man was handsome and strong and good-natured. He could have had any girl he wanted. Half of them would have given a right arm to date him; maybe both arms. "Honestly, son?"

"I felt sorry for her, Reverend. Seemed like she needed a man and didn't really care who. We only went out a half-dozen times before I knew our relationship wasn't going to work."

The air definitely felt cooler now as a soft breeze wafted through the hangar. Park could have had Becca anytime he wanted. Bobby knew that. But he chose not to. Seeing that kind of strength made Bobby's insides feel hollow. Made him wish he were a better man. He didn't deserve to be breathing the same air as Park.

"You're a good man, son."

Park shifted, and the oil barrel squeaked against the concrete. "So, were you the father?"

It was too bad Park had to even ask him that question. After all the lies, the excuses, the hiding, it was time for the truth to be known once and for all. "No, son. I can't have kids. Me and LilliFay tried for a while, then just gave up. Never did find out the problem." The smell of motor oil and hayseed and grinding metal mingled there in the hangar, in the fading light of day.

"If it wasn't me and it wasn't you, then who was it?" Park asked.

"That's a good question." Time would tell, once the doctors finished the autopsy, of course. With modern technology, there had to be a way to determine the father of the baby in Becca's womb. Not that he wanted to think about it, but somewhere there was another man in the picture. A man who knew Becca as well as they both did. "Maybe we should ask your uncle about the autopsy report."

"He'll be interested to know you weren't the father, Reverend. People say a lot of things in this town. Half of them aren't true."

Bobby glanced away, knowing full well most people in town would go to their graves thinking he had impregnated Becca Cooper. That he was the one to try and erase his mistake on a lonely, overgrown bayou. "I'll tell you something." Maybe it didn't matter anymore. He knew his heart, and the Lord knew. "I would've loved that baby if it was mine."

The words lingered in the silence. Somewhere, there was a man who obviously didn't feel the same way. A stranger, perhaps. But more likely, someone they both knew. Maybe knew well. As the realization slowly dawned on Bobby, his face began to warm all over again.

"Hey, there."

Kelsey tried to look toward the sound, but pain shot through her neck, immobilizing her. She had landed in a sea of white: white walls, white ceiling, something soft and white surrounding her head.

"You took a nasty bump." The voice continued to speak from somewhere beside her. She strained again, and out of the corner of her eye, something dark appeared. A form, hovering just above the white sheet.

"Ouch." It was all she could think of to say, and it came out muffled, raw.

She pried open her eyes and watched the form come closer. Kind smile, oval glasses, weathered cheeks and chin. Sergeant Hines. Here. Wherever "here" was.

"You're in the hospital, Kelsey. You had an accident." The words worked their way through the fog in her mind.

Accident. Car. Something hard against her skull. "Am I dead?"

The sergeant chuckled, and she smelled coffee on his breath, sharp and bitter. "No, honey, you're not dead. You've been asleep, that's all."

She glanced toward the window, where sunlight streamed through the glass. Daylight. "What time is it?" She was more curious than worried.

"About nine. You came here last night. Got knocked on the noggin in the accident. Try not to talk too much."

Obediently, she shut her eyes again. Blocking out the light, the smell of coffee and disinfectant and cold metal, all rolled into one. The snowstorm of white around her. "Did I hit someone?"

Again, the sergeant chuckled, low and deep. A comforting sound. "More like you got hit. Witness said it looked like someone wanted to put you in the hospital, missy."

"Really?" A dull ache remained in the back of her skull. Shutting her eyes against the light wasn't working, so she opened them again.

"We need to figure out who did this to you," he said. "Mind if I ask you a few questions?"

Honestly, she felt like slipping under the covers and staying there all day. But the throbbing in her head wouldn't go away, and that made her more mad than anything else. "You bet." She winced, but forced herself to scoot up until she half-sat, half-lay on the sheets. Nobody said she had to be a martyr about it. "Could you close the blinds a bit? It's too bright. Hurts my head."

Sergeant Hines nodded, then rose and walked to the window. He pulled the drapery cord and fabric scrolled across the window, mercifully tamping the sun's rays.

She scooted higher on the pillow until she saw more of the wall and less of the ceiling. It was a hospital room, all right, and monitors, machines, and buttons of all shapes and sizes surrounded the metal bed. A soft, rhythmic beeping kept time at her side and a needle protruded from the back of her hand. "Okay."

Details emerged, one at a time. Sergeant Hines wore blue jeans and a worn work shirt. Hadn't seen him in uniform for almost a week now. She became self-conscious of the thin fabric covering her own body and pulled the covers higher on her chest. "I don't remember much, so I don't know if I can help."

"That's okay, Kelsey." Sergeant Hines pulled a notepad from the pocket of his shirt and flipped it open. "Take it slow. No one said you had to get all the details right." Next he pulled a pencil from the same pocket. "Just tell me what happened."

Kelsey shut her eyes. Easier to think without the distraction of things that buzzed and beeped. "I was coming home from work. Must have been seven o'clock or so." Renee had left, she remembered, along with the men who ran the printing press next door. Stars twinkled when she walked into the parking lot. A million stars overhead. She opened her eyes again.

"I didn't see it coming. I was driving along. The next thing I know, someone's headlights are right behind me. Practically in my backseat." She remembered wondering if the driver was drunk. "The next minute I'm sitting in someone's driveway with a steering wheel in my face." The old man who had come to her aid looked so surprised. She must have been bleeding, because his eyes looked fearful. She ran her free hand through her hair now, but felt nothing. No bandages, no tape, no gauze. "Am I cut up?" She could only imagine what kind of scars would run down her cheeks and chin.

"Calm down." The sergeant laid his hand on her shoulder. "You've got one or two scrapes on your forehead, but that's it. No blood anymore."

That was good. At least she wouldn't frighten young schoolchildren when she left the hospital.

"Did you see the car?" Sergeant Hines wrote something in the notebook.

"No, it was too dark. But . . ." The bright light had come so close; just behind her ear. "It must have been a pickup truck, because the headlights were higher than normal. Definitely above my backseat."

"Those are good details. You should've been a cop. Most people don't notice things like that."

"Most people don't write for a newspaper." She tried to smile, but that only sent pain shooting through her skull. "Ouch." Thank goodness for her journalism training. She thought it was silly when they had worked on their observation skills back in college, but now she knew why.

"I know you don't feel too good right now, but they said you can go home in a few hours." He flipped the notepad closed and returned it to his pocket. "I called Park, and he wants to pick you up. Sounded very concerned, I might add." He chuckled. "Mighty concerned. I don't know what spell you've put on my nephew, but he wanted to rush right down here in the middle of the night. I had to threaten him to make him stay away. Not that it's any of my business—"

"Which it isn't. I'd like to get fixed up a little before I see him. Not exactly looking my best, am I?"

"You've got time, child." Sergeant Hines patted her shoulder. "Rest a little more. I've got questions for you, but they can wait. Let's get you better and home where you belong."

"Do you have to go?" She felt so much better with him sitting there.

" 'Fraid so, Kelsey. I've got some investigating to do. And, you've got some resting to do."

"One more thing." She remembered the stranger's voice on the telephone. Warning her to stop writing stories about Becca's murder. A thud, pop, crash against the back of her car. Out of the blue. Or, maybe not. "I got a telephone call yesterday morning. Must have forgotten to tell you about it out on the bayou. Someone told me not to cover Becca Cooper's murder any more. He said I'd be sorry."

"Hmmm. Do you have that reverse calling feature at work?"

"Reverse what?" Even simple words took a while to unscramble now. A second's delay before they sorted themselves out. "No, I don't think so. Our stuff's pretty basic. But you think it's the same person, right?"

He nodded. "Could be. You need to rest now, and I've got some leads to check out. Let's both do what we have to do, okay?"

With that, he turned to leave and she let her head sink back into the pillow. Into the warm cocoon of fluff, devoid of color and light and sound. She had started to drift off to sleep again, when an unfamiliar voice pierced through the fog in her mind.

"Miss Garrett?"

Kelsey pried her eyes open to find a woman staring down at her. An older woman, with a smooth round face and twinkling eyes. "Hmmm?"

"You need to sit up, honey," the woman told her. "Doctor wants one more X-ray before you go home."

The last thing Kelsey wanted to do was sit up. She'd spent what little energy she had talking to Sergeant Hines, and now all she wanted was a few more hours of mindless slumber. Couldn't the nurse see that? "Please go away." She hoped the woman would sympathize with her plight and leave her alone.

"Doctor's orders, dear. This won't take long. We're going to put you into a wheelchair and take you to radiology."

Kelsey groaned. When she felt something shift beneath her, she knew she definitely wasn't dreaming. In fact, a man had joined the nurse at the bedside, and he carefully lowered the guardrails on her bed. In one swift motion, he slid her from the sheets into a wheelchair, while the nurse removed the needle from her arm.

Like a rag doll in the middle of a tea party, Kelsey let the duo wheel her from the room and into a hallway. The minute they passed the transom, she felt chilled. The nurse's assistant must have read her mind, because he reached around and retrieved a thin blanket from the foot of the bed, which he draped over her knees. Then he silently took control of the wheelchair from the nurse and moved her farther into the hall.

Everything passed in a blur. Several closed, double-wide doors. A square bulletin board holding "tip sheets" for the staff. Finally, another square, this one a sign announcing the radiology department and a series of small, cave-like rooms. They stopped in front of the third room, where the technician spoke a few words to a woman standing by a putty-colored machine. He nodded toward Kelsey, then disappeared as quietly as he had come.

"Head trauma, possible concussion, no contusions." The woman appeared to be speaking to Kelsey, but her eyes remained focused on a slim chart she held in her hand. "Got banged up pretty good, did you?"

Kelsey nodded as the technician helped her rise from the wheelchair and sit on the lip of the machine. The long tube reminded her of an unwrapped soda can lying on its side, with the impossibly small opening at its head serving as the popped top on the can. "I don't suppose you have an open-air version of this?" She knew she was being irrational, but the opening didn't seem large enough to accommodate her shoulders, let alone her whole body.

"You're having a brain scan. This kind has a stronger magnet so the doctor can get a better view."

Kelsey shrugged and lay on the table, still not convinced. After all she'd been through, though, a simple test seemed like the least of her worries. "Okay then."

The technician placed a small device in her lap, hard and cold. "Hold onto this," she told her. "If you feel uncomfortable at any time during the test, press the button and I'll stop the machine."

Kelsey clutched at the button with both hands. When the technician disappeared and the lights dimmed, she tried to relax by closing her eyes and imagining she was back in the bland hospital room, with nothing more exciting to look at than the beige ceiling tiles overhead. After all she'd been through over the past day, the image of pure white walls and clutter-free surfaces was deeply soothing. She didn't even mind when the noise began; a dull grinding noise that resonated in her ears and seemed to intensify the farther she moved through the tunnel.

Just like the noise of the truck inching up behind her the night before. The low, grinding sound of metal against metal. Right before the first crack into her rear bumper. She flinched on the table, determined to keep her thumbs off of the button lying on her stomach, to let the test continue regardless of her jittery reflexes.

Another second or two passed. Still, the noise wouldn't abate as gears shifted around her head, creating a wind-tunnel effect that left her disoriented and confused. What was that by her left ear? Unable to resist any longer, she depressed the button in her hand, finally exhaling when her finger touched the cool plastic.

Nothing. The machine continued to churn around her, the noise continued to fill her ears, her skull, her brain. Maybe she hadn't pressed hard enough. Kelsey inhaled deeply, then pressed the button one more time, convinced the gigantic machine around her would now stop its nauseating revolutions. Again, nothing. The whine continued to echo around her, growing even louder. Her heart jumped. The button wasn't working. The safety measure the technician had so reassuringly laid in her lap wasn't working. Worst of all, she couldn't catch her breath, and she gulped in the air greedily, like a starving child brought in to a banquet.

One heart-stopping second later, the machine ground to a halt, the echo softening bit by bit until she heard only the wonderful sound of silence as the table beneath her began to extract her from the monstrous contraption.

"I'm so sorry!" The technician looked clearly flustered as she laid her hands on Kelsey's shoulders and looked into her eyes. "It was the only chance I had to use the restroom. Are you okay?"

No, Kelsey wanted to scream, she was not okay, but seeing the woman's panic-stricken face somehow caused her own heart rate to slow. After all, here she was, back in the open air and able to breathe again. "Fine," she mumbled. Turning to look back at the machine that had spit her out of its miniscule mouth, she felt silly now. It was just a machine. One click and the tech had doused its drone, its churning, psychedelic spinning. One click and she was fine. "Put me back in."

The technician shook her head. "Even though it's not as strong as a brain scan, I think we should wait for your doctor to order an open-air MRI. Let's get you back to your room."

"No, it'll take too long." Kelsey shook her head as she spoke. "I'm not staying here an hour longer than I have to. Please let me finish the test."

The tech looked at her askance. "Are you sure? I heard you on that buzzer. You were in full panic mode."

Kelsey steeled herself and released the buzzer from the death grip her fingers had encapsulated it in. "If the doctor needs this test before I can go home, I want to finish now. I won't use the buzzer this time. Promise."

"I probably shouldn't let you, after the way you used that thing." The tech glanced around the darkened room. "You have to promise you won't use it again, okay? I'll give you some earplugs, and that will drown out the noise. A lot of people can't stand the noise."

Kelsey watched the woman reach into a pocket on her smock and withdraw a pair of earplugs wrapped in cellophane. She gave them to Kelsey, who popped one into her right ear, then her left, and lay back down on the hard surface. When her head touched the plastic, she gave the technician the "thumbs-up" sign and closed her eyes. No matter how long this took, whether or not she felt as if she was suffocating, she was going to finish this test.

Only by finishing the MRI did she have any chance of being discharged and released to the waiting arms of Park. Not to mention her newfound friends like Sergeant Hines, Bernie, even Renee. They would be worried about her, which gave her the strength to lie on the table, inert, without once touching the buzzer in her palm. Not once. Her eyes remained closed as she thought about the people who waited for her beyond the hospital, the people who wanted her to come home. Her home.

A short while later, LilliFay arrived at the police station. The glass door fronting it needed a good scrubbing, she noticed, because cobwebs hung in the corners like silver moss. Honestly, give the place to men to look after and see what happened? Course, they had a female officer, but she couldn't be held accountable for all of them.

LilliFay swung open the door and bustled into the lobby, her sights set on Sergeant Hine's desk. Now that she'd had a chance to sleep on it, she knew she had to share Velma's story with the police department. Even if it didn't make a lick of difference to the outcome of the investigation, Sergeant Hines should know about the argument—apparently violent—in the choir loft just a pinch before Becca's death.

She paused. The landfill that passed for the sergeant's desk area had been swept clean. All traces of him were gone. Where were the folders piled ten deep? The deer head nailed to the wall, which always gave her the creeps? The ashtray with its pile of butts and quarters for the soda machine? Gone. All of it, gone.

"Morning, LilliFay." Sergeant Hines walked up behind her. In blue jeans and a work shirt, no less.

"What's going on, George? You taking a holiday?" First spiderwebs amassing on the glass door. Now this.

"Guess you didn't hear." Sergeant Hines rounded the partition and sidled up to the coffee machine, still very much at home. "I'm officially retired. Finally a free man."

"Go on. You've been here as long as I have. What do you mean, you're retired?" It would be just like George Hines to play a practical joke on her. And with her coming all this way on official police business. *Shame on him.*

"It's true. Had to leave the force, or they would've taken away my pension." He lifted the coffee pot and swirled around its contents. "Not gonna miss Earline's coffee, that's for sure." He sniffed the carafe, then put it back on the burner. "I'd offer you some, but that might be assault with a deadly weapon."

LilliFay tried not to smile. "In case you don't know, George, I'm here on official police business." She nodded toward the desk in the back and the stool nearby. "This could take a while."

"By all means." He waved his hand toward the back of the room.

They walked to the sergeant's desk and LilliFay settled herself regally on the stool. "No wonder people don't like to come in here," she complained. "This thing's hard as a rock."

"Most times it's criminals who sit there, so it doesn't bother me too much."

LilliFay flinched, then ran her hand under her skirt, along the stool's seat, just to be safe. "I do hope they have a jumpsuit on or something when they come in here. Wouldn't want to pick up anything contagious."

"You were saying?" Sergeant Hines sat in the armchair behind the desk, obviously unconcerned about her health and well-being.

"Well . . . I had a visitor last night." Little did he know how rare that visit was. She still couldn't believe she'd opened the door to find Velma standing on her front porch, half melted by the blazing sun. "Told me a story I thought you'd find interesting."

"Go on. Tell me the story, LilliFay."

She gathered her thoughts, rather enjoying the attention. Most times she didn't have anything near this exciting to talk about. People only wanted to hear from her Bobby whenever she went into town. But not now. For once, she was the one who had something interesting to say.

"LilliFay? You were going to tell me the story."

"Oh, yes." She slipped her purse off her shoulder and settled it onto the floor. The purple one, of course, her favorite. "Turns out Becca Cooper was arguing with someone a couple days before her death. Velma had been looking for the church bulletins, but they were nowhere to be found."

LilliFay's fingers flew to her lips, but the name had already escaped. So much for her promise not to drag Velma into this.

"Who was it?"

"Some man, but it wasn't Bobby." She had no choice but to continue. Thankfully, the sergeant didn't ask her how Velma knew it wasn't Bobby.

"The man had his back to Velma," she continued, "so Velma didn't get a good eyeful. But they were cussing and fighting something awful." LilliFay could just imagine Velma cowering in the corner at the sound of all that swearing. This time, though, her timidity had paid off because Velma witnessed something no one else had been privy to.

"Did she have any idea at all who the man was?"

LilliFay scooted forward on the stool, eager to continue. "She didn't see his face, but he was wearing a starched white work shirt and had gray hair." There. Those were good details. Sure enough, Sergeant Hines jotted something else onto a notepad he'd pulled from his pocket.

"But not Bobby, huh?"

Truth be told, that description did suit her husband. But Velma had specifically said starched white dress shirt. Her

Bobby always wore his suit coat. Said if he wanted to be known as the leader of the church, he had to look like a leader. That man always did know how to dress.

"LilliFay . . . I asked how she knows it wasn't Bobby."

There he went again, rushing her. "Because Bobby always wears his suit coat. Plus, she would have known by the back of his head. You don't work for a person for thirty years without knowing what they look like from behind."

"You have a point. So, what do you think about all this?"

LilliFay blinked. It'd been a while since she'd been asked that question. He genuinely wanted to know what she thought. The realization made her feel good inside. "I think it was someone who worked at the church, but maybe not a staff person. There are plenty of other people who come through the sanctuary. Volunteers, all of them."

"Like who?"

Again, he stared at her as if he couldn't wait to hear her response. She straightened even more. "There's ushers. Deacons. Sunday School teachers. That's just the start."

Sergeant Hines nodded. "Interesting. Very interesting. Anyone in particular you think we could start with?"

"I say we start with the deacons. Harris Zeff would know who was at the church. He'll tell us who we should talk to."

Sergeant Hines flipped the notepad closed. "Good idea. I'll drive us over to his place if you promise to behave yourself."

"Oh, no. I'm not getting in your squad car again." She lifted her purse from the floor and rose. "I'll drive. It's not like I haven't gone that way a million times before. Besides, I *know* who's been in *my* car."

The sergeant rose, too. "I can't even drive the squad car anymore." He waved toward the lobby of the police station. "Try to drive more than twenty miles an hour, though."

"Why, sergeant. If only everybody were as law-abiding as I

am, we'd have a lot less trouble in this town." With that, Lilli-Fay sashayed into the lobby, sweeping past the forlorn-looking coffee pot and the door with its spidery moss.

Cardboard boxes surrounded Bobby as he stood in his office, hands on hips. Amazing how quickly objects multiplied over thirty years. Most of the stuff was out-of-date—clunky audio-cassettes, old bulletins, ledgers filled with budgets from decades gone by. Like an archaeologist who sifts through rubble for treasure, once in a while he pulled out something meaningful. A proclamation from the mayor of Enterprise. Thank-you cards from the orphanage the church sponsored overseas. Even a transcript from one of his radio broadcasts. Things he might actually keep. The rest could be stored away until he found a new church home. That is, if he and LilliFay ever found a new church home.

In truth, he was old enough to retire. Even eligible for a pension from the Association of Charismatic Churches. The pension wouldn't make him and LilliFay rich, but it would allow them to buy a condo in Sun City, Nevada, and end their days on a quiet note. For once, he could stay up late on a Saturday night and sleep in the next morning. What did it feel like to rise after the sun, to walk down a street and not have someone call your name? To sit in a barbershop and read a magazine, unencumbered by someone else's troubles? To remain anonymous in a crowded room?

He'd soon find out. He placed a dog-eared thesaurus in the last box and folded the lid in on itself. A man's life reduced to a dozen moving boxes and a monthly pension check. He lifted the box half-heartedly, but stopped when his lower back complained. Maybe Park Daniels could load these things in his pickup and bring them to LilliFay for him. She'd grouse, but she'd find a spot in the attic and maybe even pull out a few pictures to put on the walls. That was the thing about LilliFay. She could keep herself busy, no matter what. He only hoped he could do the same.

Something moved near the door to his office and a stranger poked his head inside. The stranger looked to be down on his luck. His t-shirt had a torn collar and his forearms were scratched raw. Probably another transient hitchhiking through Enterprise on his way to Houston.

"Can I help you, son?" Odds were the good the man wanted a handout or a hot meal, and Bobby'd provide what he could.

"You the pastor here?"

Bobby straightened and laid his arm across the box. It must look odd to see a man his age trying to wrestle with a box this size. "Yes, I am. Can I help you?"

"Do you have anything to eat?" The stranger glanced around the room as if a sandwich might magically appear. Brushy brows shrouded his eyes, which looked haunted.

"No, son. But we can get you fixed up." No matter what, God's children deserved a little kindness. He reached for his wallet and withdrew a few bills. "How long has it been since you've had something to eat?"

The stranger stepped forward and snatched the cash from his hand as if Bobby might change his mind. In a flash, he wadded the money up and shoved it into his jeans, which hung low on his skinny hips. "Yesterday." He said it without a trace of sadness or despair. As if everyone ate only once a day.

"Go on over to the Grande Burrito on Fifth Street. The food's good, and it'll fill you up. Tell Bernie I sent you."

"Oh, no." The stranger shook his head. "Can't do that."

Bobby replaced the wallet in his back pocket. He was used to strangers coming to church and asking him for money. What he wasn't used to was having to argue with them about where to spend it. Better for the man buy a burrito and a soda from Bernie than a six-pack of malt liquor from Midway Liquors. "Course you can, son. Bernie will make you feel right at home. He doesn't care what you're dressed like."

Again, the man shook his head. "That dude said I could work for him. Spent a couple hours washing dishes there yesterday."

It didn't surprise Bobby one bit him that Bernie would offer a homeless person a job. Bernie was good people, too. Didn't care what a person looked like, or smelled like, or how they talked, he would welcome a stranger the same as a friend. "He won't mind, son. If you don't mind me asking, though, why'd you quit?" While he was all for helping the less fortunate, he also believed in good old-fashioned work. God helped those who helped themselves.

"Dunno. Didn't seem like something I'd be good at. Man, I just want to get to Mexico."

Bobby winced. Only fugitives and tourists headed that far south, and this man didn't look like a tourist. Bobby wasn't one to aid and abet a felon, that was for sure. "Are you in trouble with the law?" As a man of the cloth, he felt obligated to keep many secrets but only if they didn't involve breaking the law.

"Nah. Ever since I got kicked out of school I kinda moved around. Been to Tulsa, Chicago, New Orleans. Figure as long as it's only me, it doesn't much matter where I go."

"No family, then?" Which was sadder . . . the way the stranger slumped, hands in pockets, a hang-dog expression on his face, or the fact that no one on earth was there to claim him? It didn't seem right one way or the other.

"Nope. Never been married. Never even came close. Hard to meet someone when you're on the road." Several teeth were missing from the stranger's smile.

Bobby reached behind him and withdrew his wallet again. This time, he took out a $100 bill he had tucked into the back flap for emergencies. LilliFay always reminded him that he never knew when it might come in handy. Though he was about to find out what life was like on a pension, giving this man the hundred only seemed right. "Here you go."

The young man's eyes widened as, slowly, he accepted the bill. This time, he didn't wad it up and stuff it into his pocket though. He carefully folded it into thirds and tucked it into his left shoe. "Bless you, man."

Amazing how life happened. For all Bobby knew, the dirty man standing in front of him had been sent by God to be an angel on earth. Now that Becca was gone and LilliFay had granted him grace, who was Bobby to deny another person? "No. God bless you."

The man turned to leave, his shoulders a tad straighter now. He left the office as quietly as he had come, like a vapor that disappeared into thin air.

Bobby sighed and left the room a moment later, as well. There was so little left to do, and none of it seemed important now. The church would go on as it always had, as it always would, whether or not he was there to guide it.

He made his way down the hall and paused before the opening to the sanctuary. The church doors had been thrown open wide, and midday sun illuminated the space. The sight of gleaming pews and majestic stained glass windows always took his breath away. No matter how many times he stood at the threshold of the sanctuary, no matter how many times he stared at the scene of Christ on the cross before him, he would always come away awed.

He wandered through the door and began to pace down the long aisle, toward the front of the room. Memories overwhelmed him. The yowls of newborns dressed in white bonnets and lace gowns as they protested being placed in his arms for their christenings. The opening strains of the wedding march as yet another young bride approached her beaming groom. The heavy strains of organ music as black-suited men hoisted a casket onto their shoulders. These walls—and he—had witnessed it all.

"Reverend?"

He glanced to his right and saw Velma, sitting in a church pew as if it were the most natural thing in the world. She was the only one sitting in a space built for hundreds on this hot May afternoon. He'd never known her to venture into the church on a weekday before.

"Were you looking for me?"

"No." She perched on the edge of her pew, so fragile and small. Surrounded by the grandeur of the gleaming mahogany, the soaring glass, the shiny candelabra, she seemed very small, indeed. "I came here to pray."

"Mind if I join you?" He walked to her side, then edged past her into the pew. The bench squeaked as he settled onto it, the only sound in the massive space. They stared straight ahead at the picture of Christ on the cross, the Savior's head bent in anguish, his body bruised and bloodied. Finally, Bobby turned to face her. "I'm going to miss this place." Maybe it was the stillness or the majesty of it all, but he reached across and placed his hand on top of Velma's. "And you, too." Lightly, he squeezed her aged fingers, something he had never done before. Her hand felt warm and thin and very delicate.

"I'm going to miss you, too, Reverend." When she looked his way, he saw a tear at the corner of her eye. Dear, sweet Velma.

"We've had a long run, haven't we?" No doubt about it. The two of them had put in three decades together. Long enough to see the church grow from a few hundred people to thousands on special occasions, like Christmas and Easter. So many church meetings, volunteer breakfasts, Vacation Bible Schools. Too many to count, really. "I hope you like the next pastor. There are plenty of fine ones out there."

Velma shook her head, freeing the tear to roll down her cheek. "Oh, no. I couldn't work for anyone else. I'm going to retire, too."

He tightened his grip on her hand just a bit. Not too much, for he feared he'd crush her delicate fingers, but enough to let her know how deeply he appreciated that sentiment. It touched him to his very core. "You don't have to leave on my account, Velma."

"But I do." She dabbed at the tear with her free hand, erasing it from her cheek. "No one else would treat me as good as you. I don't know that I've ever told you this, Reverend. But it's been an honor to work for you."

Bobby hung his head, shame washing over him. Just like the night before, when he'd stood in the airplane hangar and acknowledged that Park Daniels was more virtuous than he ever could hope to be. "Don't say that. I let you down. I know I did."

"You let yourself down. That I can believe. We expected too much of you. I don't think any of us realized how much this church took out of you." She continued to wipe at the tear, though it was long gone. "Why, look at you now. Your hair's as gray as your trousers. It's partly my fault. I should have seen to it that you took better care of yourself. That fling with you-know-who was your way of trying to cope with everything. I know that now."

Bobby's hand dropped to the pew. Amazing how people could surprise you after you'd spent almost three decades together. "You're a kind woman. Too kind. I won't make excuses for my behavior." In truth, there were none. Nothing he could say would make up for the way he'd tarnished the reputation of the church and his own daddy's good name. "Tell me something, Velma." He knew how much she disliked Becca Cooper. Disliked her enough never even to utter her name, always calling her "you-know-who" or "that girl." Couldn't bring herself to acknowledge Becca's existence, when he was the one who had started their affair.

"Who do you think killed her, Velma?" While he couldn't imagine Velma having anything to do with Becca's murder, she'd been around long enough to hear and see things most people weren't privileged to. Decades' worth of mumbles . . . closed doors . . . secrets.

"I honestly don't know, Reverend." She studied the stained glass figure of Christ, first the sandals on his feet, then the top of the savior's head. "I thought about doing that girl harm only once. That was back when all of your foolishness with her first started. I thought that if I got her to go back to Oklahoma, that would take care of everything. Wanted to threaten her . . . really, I did . . . but I knew it was none of my business."

Bobby remembered that day, early on, when Becca came to his office in tears. Told him she'd thought about returning to Oklahoma and said something about the wickedness in this town. He didn't understand what she was talking about then.

"Tell you this, though. Much as I wanted that girl gone, I never would have lifted a finger against her. I learned my lesson when I hurt those poor babies in Vacation Bible School."

"What do you mean?"

"You don't know this, Reverend, but it used to make me so mad when they wouldn't sit still and listen to the Good Book. It was terribly disrespectful the way they'd mess around. I used to thump them on their knuckles to get their attention, but one time I must have been too harsh."

Bobby remained silent, surprised to see such sorrow on Velma's face over something that had to have happened at least a decade ago.

"I broke one little boy's thumb. Can you imagine? I felt so bad after that, I couldn't show my face for the longest time."

"Velma, you know what you did was wrong. Why didn't you come to me?"

"I was so ashamed; afraid you'd think I was a monster. The point is, that little boy forgave me even after what I'd done to him. His name was Shawn, and I'll never forget that. Ever. People will forgive you, too, Reverend. I know they will."

Bobby remained in the pew with Velma for the longest time. She was like a sister to him. They'd started together, lo, those many decades ago, and now they were going to end together. May God have mercy on them both.

He rose to leave. "Close the door on your way out, would you? I don't think I have the heart to do it just now. Oh, and here are my keys. I don't think I'll be needing them anymore."

CHAPTER 15

A little bit before one, a nurse came to help Kelsey change out of her hospital gown and into street clothes. Lucky for her, the scan had come back clean, so she was good to go as soon as her ride showed up.

When her ride appeared in the doorway, he held a large bouquet of pink tulips and had a big smile on his handsome face. As always, Park wore blue jeans smudged with motor oil and scuffed work boots. Such a sight for sore eyes.

"Park!" She hadn't meant to squeal. He walked in and placed the flowers in her lap. He smelled like motor oil and packed earth, jute ropes and cold steel. Gently, she touched a petal. "They're beautiful." She turned her face toward his for a quick kiss, mindful of the nurse watching them from the corner.

"Have to ride in the wheelchair," the nurse told them.

"The thing doesn't have any wings, but I think I can manage all right." Park took the wheelchair from the nurse and brought it to Kelsey's bedside, then lifted her up and deposited her into the chair.

"No fancy moves, okay? I've already been banged up enough for one week." She grinned, so thankful to be leaving the snowstorm of white.

"Can't promise," he teased, as he wheeled her out of the room.

She'd only looked in a mirror once that morning, to gauge the purple and yellow bruise covering her forehead, and she raked her fingers through her hair now. "I must look a mess," she said, hoping he'd disagree.

"Quite the contrary, Kelsey. For someone who just spent the night in the hospital you look damn good."

He wheeled her through the lobby and into bright sunshine and clouds overhead. She gulped in air, hungry for natural light and a warm breeze. "So good to get out of there. If you ask me, hospitals are way too sterile."

He laughed. "I think that's the point. Here. Let's get you up in the cab." Gently, he lifted her from the chair, pushed it aside, then opened the door to the pickup and placed her in the front seat.

"I'm not crippled, you know. It was just a little accident. No big deal."

"Hmmm." He joined her in the truck and fired up the engine. "Delusional, all right. The doctor told me to watch out for that."

She swatted at him, then leaned back against the cool leather headrest. They drove along the bumpy roads in companionable silence. Every once in a while, she rubbed a flower petal between her thumb and forefinger, enjoying the feel of the silky petal. "Thank you again for the flowers. You didn't have to do that."

"Let me ask you something, Kelsey." He glanced her way, turning suddenly serious. "You don't seem very comfortable when I try to take care of you. Why's that?"

She shrugged. "I don't know. Maybe I'm afraid you'll think I'm weak. That I can't take care of myself."

"It's what we do around here . . . we help each other." He reached across the seat and took her hand. "You don't have to be defensive. I know you can take care of yourself."

"Thanks. It might take me a while, though. I've been on my own so long, it's pretty much all I know."

They held hands all the way to the cottage, only shifting

when they pulled into her driveway. Without thinking, she automatically pushed open the door, which caused Park to groan.

"At least let me get the door!"

She waited while he walked around to her side of the pickup and helped her step from the running board to pavement. At the last second, he swooped her into his arms and carried her up the walk, the tulips swaying with each step.

In one fluid motion, he pulled her house key from her pocket, unlocked the door, swung her through the foyer, and deposited her on the living room couch. In contrast to the bright daylight, the house seemed dark and lonely. He flicked on a lamp, and when he placed a pillow under her head, she asked, "Can you—"

Before she could finish the sentence, though, he took the bouquet from her arms and walked into the kitchen.

"Lower left cabinet," she yelled from the living room, guiding him as if they'd known each other all of their lives. She rested her head against the pillow, feeling silly to be lying down again. It had to be mid-afternoon by now, and all this resting was making her feel lazy. She swung her legs over the side of the sofa and sat up. There was the pile of magazines on the coffee table, still unread. The mismatched chairs she'd acquired from here and there, hoping they looked more shabby-chic than working-girl poor. The oil painting she'd found at a flea market of a woman writing at a desk. There wasn't much to show off in the room, but at least it was all hers.

Park walked back to the living room and set the flowers, which he'd placed in an old tin can with a few cupfuls of water, on the coffee table. "Am I going to have to tie you down?"

Kelsey smirked. Not such a bad image to think about, after all. "I'm not an invalid. I can manage just fine."

He picked up the television remote from the arm of the couch and laid it in her lap. "One afternoon. That's all I'm asking.

Take a nap or something. I'll check on you tonight."

"Do you have to leave?" Having him in the house changed everything. Made it feel like a home. She'd miss that.

" 'Fraid so." He brushed her hair back from her cheek. "Might have another contract in the Gulf of Mexico, and I need to meet the bosses back at the hangar."

Watching her, he must have sensed how she felt, because he was quick to add, "I promise I'll be back. Give me a few hours. Three, tops." She nodded and he kissed the crown of her head. "Don't do anything. Just sit there and behave, okay?"

He started for the door, but before he opened it, he turned and wagged a finger at her. "I mean it. No getting off that couch."

"Aye, aye. I'll be here when you get back, sir."

"You're a handful, all right."

The minute he left the room, the house fell silent. Too silent. She put aside the remote. This would never do. No matter what, she couldn't spend her day locked inside like an invalid. Not with everything happening back in town.

The floor swayed a bit as she rose, but she straightened anyway. She'd promised Park she would still be on the couch when he returned. Between now and then, though, was another story.

For one thing, she hadn't spoken to Renee since the day before. Heaven only knew what kind of backlog awaited her at the newsroom. She shuffled through the foyer, glimpsing her reflection in the mirror as she passed. An enormous bruise fanned over her forehead, more yellow than blue now. No telling how long she'd have that reminder of her little adventure on the road.

She waited a good five minutes for Park to drive away, then made her way to her car, which was sitting at the curb. Ugly dents striated the bumper and the paint had been scraped clean.

It would be a miracle if the car started at all, but it fired up when she inserted the key.

It felt odd to drive through town, glancing every second or so into her rearview mirror. She feared someone would speed up behind her again. Always checking for a car behind her, unable to resist the pull of the mirrored glass. She crossed the intersection at the end of her street without incident, though, and pulled cautiously into the right-hand lane. After driving for a mile or so, she finally began to relax and allowed herself to glance around. So nice to see the tree swings, the lush lawns, the hound dogs lounging in the shade. Just another late spring day in Enterprise, Texas. She rolled down her window to lure a breeze in.

Halfway to the newsroom, she passed a construction cone, then another. A line of bright orange cones trailed down Main Street, blocking her route. Not a single workman appeared, but the cones were impassable. She turned right, onto a side street, hoping to navigate all back roads to the *Country Caller*. A mile or so down, she pulled to the side of the road, suddenly disoriented. She'd never come this way before. Plus, a dull ache throbbed at the base of her skull.

Maybe she should have listened to Park, after all. He'd warned her not to get off the couch. Now, here she was, lost only a few miles from the newsroom and with a wicked headache, to boot.

A chain-link fence ran along the right side of the car, signaling the start of someone's property. It looked like every other mini-ranch on the outskirts of Enterprise: red brick house, shingled roof, white metal carport instead of an enclosed garage. The kind of place country folks bought if they wanted to work in town. Maybe raise a few cows and sheep, have a chance to live near the city, but still feel a million miles away.

She'd forgotten to grab her cell phone from the kitchen table, and she needed help. Park might be angry if she tried to reach him, but she could count on Renee to guide her back to the newsroom safely without asking any questions.

She parked the car on the side of the road, and stepped from it to a gravel path. If there was one good thing about living in a small Southern town—and she was coming to find there were many good things about it—it was that no one would think twice if she asked to borrow a phone. In fact, plenty of folks still left their front doors unlocked, either because they knew their neighbors or they figured no one would be so mean-spirited as to take something that didn't actually belong to them.

A path meandered to the front porch, past an American flag wavering in the tepid breeze. The path ended at a raised porch with a lattice-work skirt, some potted plants scattered here and there. This particular property had several outbuildings, too, including a tool shed in back and a second metal carport, almost hidden by the fence-line of pin oaks.

The dilapidated carport held an old pickup. It would be impossible to see it from the road, and the sight of it stopped Kelsey cold.

The hidden truck had a crumbled front bumper streaked with bright red paint. The exact red of her trusty compact. Kelsey shook her head to clear the fog. *Impossible.* She took another step and looked again. No, she wasn't seeing things. The vehicle in the carport wore streaks of orange-red, which her owner's manual had dubbed "candy apple." Either she was delusional from the pain meds, or the truck that had rammed into her bumper the night before sat only yards away.

She faltered. How could it be that this quaint brick farm-house, with its American flag and lattice-work porch, sheltered such a menacing vehicle?

A pair of feet shot out from the undercarriage of the battered pickup. The appendages wore scuffed cowboy boots splayed in a "V." Before she could react, their owner slid out from the undercarriage, as well, on a padded dolly. A can of paint thinner and an old bath towel lay nearby.

The man stared at her. It was Harris Zeff, the deacon at Second Coming Charismatic Church. Wearing oil-splattered work clothes, his hair wild around his head, a wrench in his hand. As he rose to meet her, she saw a smudge of grease on his nose and smelled the pungent odor of gasoline.

"Hello, Miss Garrett," he said, with a wave of the wrench.

As she stood there in the hot sun, the dull ache racking the back of her skull, she grasped for something, anything to say. "I was passing by. Don't have my phone. They're doing construction on Main Street."

"Are they really?" He carefully wiped the wrench against his coveralls. With a casual flick of his wrist, he pointed it toward the beat-up pickup. "Crashed into my tractor last week. Think I'd know better than to park in a blind spot. You were saying?"

"Oh." The truck's reddened bumper looked so similar to her car's. The marks looked fresh, too.

"C'mon inside. You can borrow my phone. Might even have some banana bread left over." He gripped her elbow. "Since you're here, you might as well visit for a while."

Nothing stirred in the ranch house. "No. Really. I . . . I should get back to work," she stammered. The ground seemed to sway under her. Maybe it was the medication or the pain that pulsed against her skull, but she felt ready to faint. Right there, on an unfamiliar lawn in front of a house she'd never seen before. "Maybe you could bring the phone out here?"

He tightened his grip. "Oh, no, come on now. Let's go inside for a minute or two. I'm sure that newspaper of yours will manage just fine." He pulled her toward the empty house. "Say, you've got a nasty bruise there. Let's get you a warm washcloth while we're at it."

LilliFay did her best to drive the car more than thirty miles an hour, though it wasn't easy with the construction cones that blocked the road. Honestly, couldn't they work on Main Street at night and be less bothersome for honest folks trying to do a little business in town?

She swerved around the first cone and felt the weight of George's stare. "There's no one out here, George. If they're going to block the road, they should at least be doing their job."

The second cone proved a little trickier and she jerked the steering wheel a bit harder than she wanted.

"LilliFay." George glared at her, as if it was her fault she had to drive in fits and starts down the biggest road in town.

"What? Last I checked this was my car. Figure I can drive it however I choose."

She swerved around the final cone, narrowly avoiding it, and swung into the first open parking space she found, right in front of the insurance agency. "See? Best parking space in town."

With that, she smoothed her hair back and reached behind her for the purple purse. "Let's keep my driving our own little secret. Like you said, you're not on the police force anymore. Way I figure, it's better to make it here quick and in one piece than use some crazy detour."

Once LilliFay swung open the door, she stepped into hot sun. "Besides," she tucked her head in to watch the sergeant release his seatbelt, "it's their fault for not having anyone on the job."

With that, LilliFay slammed the car door and strode up the sidewalk to the storefront where Harris Zeff did his business. Thankfully, George emerged from the car soon after and followed her all the way up the steps.

"Afternoon." A receptionist looked up when she entered the office. She was that young girl Harris said he had found on the church's job board. She seemed capable enough.

"Hello. Is Harris in?" LilliFay glanced around the room. She hadn't been to Harris's place of business for quite some time. He'd decorated it like the old cowboy he was. There was a bleached cow's skull on a side table, an Indian blanket thrown over a leather armchair, an assortment of spurs and tack. Even had framed a collection of barbed wire and mounted it on the wall.

"No, ma'am. He didn't come in today. Called me this morning, said he wasn't feeling well."

"That's too bad." George spoke kindly to the young girl, as if he wanted to win her to his side. "Those summer colds can be a killer, all right. Mind if we use your phone?"

The girl waved toward Harris's desk. "Of course you can. Come on back."

She smiled brightly as they made their way to Harris's desk—a mahogany partner's desk with kneeholes in the front and back. Like the rest of the room, the area around the desk looked like a Western museum, with Indian arrowheads, cowhide lampshades, and more spurs. My, but Harris did like his Texana. LilliFay followed George to the desk, where he stopped and lifted the receiver of a heavy black telephone. Amazing it wasn't covered in cowhide, as well.

As George dialed some numbers, LilliFay poked around on an occasional table leaning against the wall. Not only was the receptionist sweet, she also dusted well, because the bric-a-brac shone under the fluorescent lights. LilliFay ran her index finger down the length of the table. Yes, indeed, that girl knew her way around a dust cloth. LilliFay bent closer, to see if maybe she'd missed some spots on the sides of the table, when she spotted a long pole protruding from the backside. A handle it was, made of steel. Curious, LilliFay withdrew the handle from its resting place and appraised her find. It was a branding iron, complete with the owner's mark at its tip.

She glanced at George. He had the strangest look on his face. "What?"

The branding iron glistened under the overheads. Splotched with crimson on its tip. Sure enough, the mark was a "Z," something Harris would use to mark his cows and separate them from anyone else's.

"Give me that." She flinched at George's command. So brusque. As if she had stolen the thing from under the table.

"It's just a branding iron." She lowered it, the dark stain unmistakable in the bright lights.

"I said . . . give me that, LilliFay." George held out his hand.

Meekly, she handed over the tool and scooted away. "No need to shout. It was on the floor. Just lying there."

George held the branding iron up, twirling it over and over in the air. He seemed mesmerized. Whatever did he see in such a common, everyday object?

"What's it mean, George?" The look on his face frightened her. Whatever he held in his hand, it carried great importance; that much she knew. "George?" Almost like he couldn't hear her question as he twirled the stick around and around in the air.

"Do you suppose there are many branding irons with this mark, LilliFay?" Finally, George stopped twirling the stick in the air.

"Probably not. Most folks don't have a name that starts with Z."

"What do you think would happen," he asked, as he finally lowered the iron to his side, "if it fell in the mud. Say, on a bayou?"

"Why, it'd leave a mark there, of course. Looks heavy enough.

Why are you asking me this, George? What difference does it make if Harris's branding iron falls in the mud?"

The sergeant still seemed lost in his own world, a thousand miles away from her and from the insurance office.

"George?" Truly, she felt frightened. "Okay, I'll just put it back. Right where it was. No one has to know."

George pulled a hankie from his pocket and shook his head. "Oh, no, LilliFay." He wrapped the hankie around the shaft of the iron with a slow, methodical movement. "If I'm right, you're looking at a murder weapon."

Of course. The ominous brown stain. The weighty branding iron, in front of her now. Images clicked into place, one after another. Kelsey Garrett's newspaper story about the way someone had bashed in Becca's skull. All those Sundays when Harris watched Becca play the piano in church. Leering at her, really. LilliFay had meant to say something to Bobby about it— really, she had—but she never could find the right time. Now this.

"Is something wrong?" The young receptionist stood behind them.

"Where's Mr. Zeff?" Sergeant Hines demanded, dropping any pretense at friendliness.

"He's at home. Like I said, sir. He didn't feel well—"

George brushed past her. "C'mon, LilliFay. We're going to the ranch. This time, I'll drive."

Kelsey nearly tripped walking up the porch stairs with Harris. She shouldn't have taken the detour to the newsroom, shouldn't have seen the battered pickup truck in the shed, shouldn't be here now, stumbling up the steps of a farmhouse with a man she barely knew, the throbbing in her head refusing to go away. Why hadn't she listened to Park?

"Careful, the wood's a little rotted here." Harris reached

around her to open a white screen door. They entered a drab sitting area, which smelled of cat hair and dust. Unlike the charming porch outside, the inside of the home was dreary, awash in grays and browns.

A faded paisley couch faced an old upright piano with a round stool. As they passed it, Kelsey noticed a hymnal had been propped open on the piano, its pages turned to one of her favorites.

Harris guided her through the sitting area and into the kitchen, which also seemed neglected. A row of dingy cabinets lined the walls, and a ripped curtain hung over the porcelain sink. In the middle of the kitchen sat a well-worn butcher's block, holding a lump of something soft and brown, and a carving knife.

Finally, Harris released her arm. When he did, she glanced over his head to a rough shelf nailed above the pantry door. A plain two-by-four, holding painted tins and a trio of porcelain figurines. Harris's eyes followed hers to the shelf.

They both noticed it at the same time. An ornate chalice, beautifully carved and plated in gold, glowing above their heads. It was much too formal for the farmhouse kitchen. It looked like the kind of chalice a church would use for the Lord's Supper. But . . . the chalice used by Second Coming had been stolen, Harris had told her. Probably by someone who was involved in Becca Cooper's murder, he'd said.

Nothing made sense as she stood there in the dusty kitchen with the smell of decay and neglect all around them.

"Well, well." Harris glanced away from the chalice to look at her. The dark mood of the room matched the look in his eyes. "Oh, Miss Garrett." Harris grabbed up the carving knife and brandished it toward her. "You should have left well enough alone."

Kelsey stepped backward and her shoulder brushed the

refrigerator. It felt so cold against her back. Ice cold. "What . . . what are you talking about?" she stammered. Her head felt ready to explode. Everything about the scene was surreal. Except for the hard, glinting knife in Harris's hand.

"Too bad you came here by yourself."

"You said someone stole that." She pointed to the shelf. "You took that from the church, didn't you?"

He chuckled, but kept the knife trained at her throat. "You're right, Miss Garrett. It's from *my* church."

He was a good foot taller than she was, and at least a hundred pounds heavier. No telling what he was capable of. Kelsey forced herself to focus on the knife, wavering in front of her face like a steel snake. "You don't want to do this."

"Oh, but I do." With that, he grabbed her arm and twisted her around, bringing her wrist painfully far up her back. He shoved her face against the refrigerator door. Now that his mouth hovered above her ear, she could smell whiskey, sour and strong.

"Let me go," she demanded. She hated being trapped between cold metal and the smell of booze. She wanted to fight back, but she knew from the many hours she'd spent reading crime reports that fighting sometimes didn't pay. No, sometimes it was better to stall until help could arrive. From what she'd read, even delaying the crime for a few minutes could be enough to save a person's life.

"Why'd you do it? Everyone told me Becca Cooper was a wonderful person. Why would you kill someone like that?"

Harris jerked her hand higher behind her back, stretching the muscles painfully, as if he meant to pull her shoulder out of its socket.

"Wonderful? She was a slut. Even slept with a man of God. She didn't deserve better."

"But she was pregnant. Didn't you care?"

Kelsey winced from the pain in her arm. One word played over and over in her mind: stall.

"You don't know anything." Harris sounded disgusted now. "Whose baby do you think it was? And don't you tell me she didn't like it when I took her like that. She was asking for it."

The tugging on her arm was almost unbearable now. Kelsey bit into her lip to keep from crying out. "You murdered your own baby?" she sputtered.

Harris spun her around, finally releasing her arm, which fell limply to her side. "Shut up! Do you hear me . . . just shut up!"

His eyes darted around the kitchen, then landed on a dish towel draped over the edge of the sink. He lunged for it, then knotted it around her wrists with a few sloppy twists and turns. "You women are all alike. Acting like you don't want it, when you know you do. Got to learn who's the boss."

She trembled at the hate in his voice. Such a black, black heart. If she was going to survive this, she'd have to depend on herself and no one else.

"I have to go to the bathroom," she lied. "Please."

Harris snorted. "Sorry, little lady. Where you're going you won't need to do that." With that, he jerked her in front of him and pushed her forward, the knife tip sharp against the small of her back. "Walk," he commanded.

Kelsey's mind raced as she moved forward. Through the living room, out the front door. She'd never make it if she tried to run. The property was set too far back from the road, and Harris would pounce on her before she got more than a few yards. She glanced at the line of pin oaks that edged the property. Very secluded, which was the reason most people bought these ranches to begin with. No telling where anyone else was at the moment. Harris's wife? Probably long gone. Traffic? No one would travel on this road unless they had a house nearby, and the nearest neighbor was a half-mile away. Construction workers? Not a chance. She'd seen how empty Main Street was when she tried to navigate to the newsroom. She walked as slowly as possible down the porch steps. One foot in front of the other, her heart pounding with each footfall. Before reaching the final step, she paused. There was no other way. Deliberately, purposefully, she tripped on the last step, the ground rushing up to meet her in a blur of brown and blue sky.

The next instant, Harris was on top of her, scrambling to pull her to her feet. She kicked him as hard she could in the groin, which sent him reeling backward, toward the porch. Thank goodness she'd remembered to flex her fingers when he tied her hands with the towel and she worked the cloth—painfully—inch by inch down her wrists, until it fell to the ground.

As she did that, Harris crashed against the latticework that covered the crawlspace. She took the porch steps two at a time and grabbed for a pot of peonies. He lunged at her, but she reached her arms overhead as far as she could and brought the clay pot crashing against his skull. The dull crack of pottery hitting hard bone rang out, and the next moment, Harris lay writhing at her feet.

The man moaned once, then nothing. Kelsey grabbed the knife from his hand anyway and steadied it above his chest. She'd knocked him out cold, all right. His eyes had rolled back to the far side of their sockets and his mouth lay slack.

Kelsey picked up the twisted dish towel and bound his limp hands tightly with it. The thing did make for a good handcuff when it was tied correctly. "You're right, Mr. Zeff," she said to the unconscious form. "We women are all alike."

Sergeant Hines knocked the second and third traffic cones over with her car, but LilliFay didn't care. What was a little plastic when there was a murderer on the loose?

As she clutched the purple handbag against her chest,

adrenaline pulsed through her veins. My, but this was exciting. Nothing like this had ever happened to her before, and she pointed eagerly to the red light ahead of them. "Floor it, George!"

He was one step ahead of her, and they sailed through the intersection, which was empty. Most of the town's folks were still at work, and school wouldn't let out for a good hour or two. They careened down Main Street, then leaned into a turn as George drove left onto a farm-to-market road. Luckily, Harris lived only a few minutes away, though he liked to brag that he came from the country. Such exaggerations on his part.

They reached the ranch in two minutes flat. As they pulled up the drive, LilliFay recognized the bright red car sitting beside the road. "That's Kelsey Garrett's," she said, pointing to the car.

George nodded. "I know." He parked and they both rushed to Kelsey's car. LilliFay peered into it, looking for what, it was hard to say. "She left her handbag on the front seat. Maybe she's only been here a minute or two."

She scurried after George, then, as he strode from the car to the chain-link fence. He pushed the gate open and held it there so she could follow him. The ranch looked good enough on the outside. Though ever since Harris's wife had died, it was hard to say how long that would last.

The house lay perfectly still, the only movement coming from a few birds chattering in the stand of oak trees Harris had planted along the fence-line. LilliFay glanced in that direction, then pulled up short. Why, what was Harris's old pickup truck doing there in the shed where the man used to keep his tack and his feed buckets? Most people kept a shed out back for things they didn't much care about, since the heat and humidity would surely eat everything alive during the summertime.

She called out to George, then pointed wordlessly to the

tumbledown carport when he turned. He must have understood her confusion, because he walked back to her side.

"Harris is home," she told him.

"I can see that." George stared at the pickup hard. "Why, look at that bumper."

She did, and saw the crumpled metal, the streaks of paint, the way the headlight had come clean from its socket. She'd never known Harris to be so careless with his possessions. Seems she didn't know a lot about the man.

"Oh, George." LilliFay glanced from the shed to the house. "Do you think he's got Miss Garrett?"

"He tried to get her yesterday, with his car." The way George explained it, it all made sense. "He ran Miss Garrett right off the road and put her in the hospital last night."

LilliFay had heard there'd been an accident out by the old Riley cottage, but she hadn't put two and two together until that moment. Amazing how quickly things were happening. Things that would have taken months before to discuss and dissect over coffee in town.

George began to half-walk, half-run to the house. An American flag hung over the porch, wavering in the breeze, fanning a bright pot of peonies. Peonies had become Bobby's favorite plant, too, over the past year. Since when did the men of Enterprise take such a liking to peonies? LilliFay wondered as she scurried to keep up with the police sergeant.

At the last second, George seemed to decide against the porch and swerved left, to the side of the house. He waved his arm, and LilliFay hurried faster and faster to keep up with him. All sorts of terrible thoughts entered her mind. What if they were too late? What if Harris had taken Kelsey somewhere, away from anyone and anything that could help her? LilliFay yelped and pulled up alongside George, which was no easy task considering she was wearing her church shoes and the crabgrass bunched beneath her feet.

Finally, they reached the back door. Instead of opening it, like she expected, George kicked in the wooden door, sending it sailing off its hinges. The noise surprised her. This was for real. This was not some action show playing on the television set, where a commercial would interrupt the show to sell her something or other. No, this was happening right in front of her face. She steeled her nerves and followed George through the open doorway. Halfway in, they both heard a crash, then the sound of something hard falling to the ground.

"What the—" George turned away from the kitchen door. In an instant, he hopped off the concrete step and landed back on the grass. LilliFay pivoted and followed him onto the lawn, forgetting all about her heels, the uneven soil, the way her purse slammed against her shin as she ran. Forgot about everything but the sound of the crash, which had come from the front lawn.

The minute she rounded the house, she understood. Harris lay on the ground with Kelsey hovering over him. The young woman had tied a dish towel around his wrists, like a cowgirl would hogtie a calf. All business. No fear, or at least none that LilliFay could see. In the next instant, Kelsey sank to the ground.

"Well, I'll be." LilliFay ran to her side. Harris had been cold-cocked all right. A sliver of drool ran from his mouth, which hung open a good two inches, and his eyes had rolled back into his head, as if he'd been dead for days. Dirt clung to his hair, his coveralls, his grease-smeared face. Such a strange and awkward scene.

Kelsey leaned back on her heels. She looked spent beyond belief. Even with the fierce glint in her eye.

"I'm okay," she told them. Such a brave young woman. Lilli-Fay wanted to believe her—believe her with all her heart—but then she saw the girl's lip tremble. A mere quiver, but her distress was unmistakable.

To heck with formalities. The girl had survived an awful, horrible ordeal. LilliFay reached down and hugged her to her chest. The girl smelled like hospital gowns and rubbing alcohol and sweat.

They remained like that for a long time, until the quake in the young woman's shoulders began to subside. Until a far-off sound caused both of them to look to the road. A truck careened onto the property, its engine roaring louder and louder. Pebbles shot out from the undercarriage on each revolution. Why, you'd have thought the house was on fire. And that the driver—Park Daniels—couldn't reach them any faster if he'd tried.

CHAPTER 16

Kelsey lifted her head from where it lay burrowed in LilliFay's shoulder. Ahead of them, a plume of dust rose from under the wheels of the pickup, which seemed hell-bent on reaching them in the shortest time possible. It was Park's truck, spitting up rocks and pebbles and dirt clods. He braked hard, then fishtailed to a stop. Everything was lost in a cloud of dust, until he reemerged a second later.

"Park!" Kelsey left LilliFay's embrace and stumbled into his arms and the smell of leather and hand soap. She'd been strong for so long. Too long. She allowed her head to fall against his chest, protected at last from the phantom feeling of a knifepoint pressed against her spine.

Without a word, Park raised her face to his. "What am I going to do with you?"

"Now, Park," LilliFay scolded from somewhere beside them. "Don't you get all worked up. This young lady hogtied Harris Zeff better than anyone else could. Even you, I'd say."

It was true. The man hadn't moved for several minutes, and the rise and fall of his chest gave the only indication he was still alive. He looked so harmless, as inert as the shards of broken pot that dirtied the ground around him.

"Good thing I paid attention in self-defense class," Kelsey said, trying to lighten the mood.

"And it's a good thing I didn't listen when they told me to turn in my gear." Sergeant Hines reached into the back pocket of his blue jeans and withdrew a pair of shiny handcuffs, which he clamped on top of the dish towel Kelsey had bound around the man's wrists. "Take her out of here," he said to Park. "She needs to rest after all of this."

Instead of taking her hand, though, like she thought he would do, Park swept her into his arms and whisked her toward the truck. She saw treetops and sky and the edge of the battered carport. Her head felt so heavy, she knew the adrenaline was starting to wear off. She could sleep for days and days and days, and never wake up. She allowed Park to place her in the truck like a child, which should have felt all wrong, but somehow didn't.

They drove away from the ranch without a backward glance. Past her car with its mangled bumper. Through a stretch of Main Street, where someone had upended a traffic cone and didn't even bother to replace it. On the back roads now, with no one for company but an occasional longhorn. They arrived at her cottage as the sun fell into the horizon in a flame of gold and red.

Park brought her from car to house much as they had come: with no words needed. He ducked into the doorway, careful to angle his body so she could move untouched through the opening. Instead of depositing her on the couch, though, he carried her into the kitchen, with its cheerful tiles, its soapy smell, its lemon walls. So good to be home.

"What would you like?" He placed her in a chair, then swung open the door to the refrigerator. "You've got some milk and bottled water in here."

"How about whiskey?" she joked. "Or pain killers?"

He pulled out the jug of milk instead. As he brought it to the table, he motioned toward the answering machine, which was sputtering. "Someone tried to call you."

Kelsey shrugged. Nothing seemed important enough to let it

interfere with this moment. "They'll call back if they need me."

He grabbed two glasses from the kitchen cabinet and settled in at her side. "Here's to you, Kelsey. I'm proud of you. You could have died out there today." He poured them both a glass of milk, which she gratefully accepted.

It was true. After all was said and done, there was no telling what Harris Zeff would have done to her. If he'd found the strength to kill Becca Cooper, he could have killed her, too. "How did you know to come looking for me?"

"Kelsey, Kelsey, Kelsey. There was no way you were going to stay here. I figured you'd head on back to work, so I went that way. The construction kind of messed me up, but then I saw your car on Harris's property."

The milk felt cold and thick and wonderful against her throat. She'd forgotten how parched she'd become. "Am I that transparent?"

" 'Fraid so."

"Did you think I was a goner?" It had taken her a while to link Harris Zeff with Becca's murder, but when she saw the battered pickup, everything fell into place. The argument in the choir room, which Velma had witnessed before the girl's death. The unusual imprint next to the body on the bayou, which she first imagined was the letter N. It had definitely been made by something heavy and deliberate and unyielding . . . something like a branding iron, which would provide Harris the perfect length to put distance between him and Becca when he committed his grisly crime.

"I didn't know what to think. I was too busy trying to reach you to do much of anything else."

"Are you surprised? Surprised it was Harris Zeff who murdered Becca?"

Park finally took a long, slow drink from his glass. "Yes and no. People react to death in strange ways. Maybe Harris was always like this, but ever since his wife died, it was like there was nothing behind his stare anymore. That doesn't excuse what he did, but it makes it a little easier to understand. Like he didn't have much to live for anyway."

"You're right . . . it doesn't give him an excuse. The judge won't think so, either. Lots of people have terrible things happen to them, and they don't commit murder like he did."

"Agreed. He'll have a lot of time to think about that now. I don't want to talk about Harris, though. I want to talk about that stubborn streak of yours and how it's gonna get you in trouble some day."

She grinned. "Or, keep me out of trouble. That's what got me through this mess."

"Heaven help the man who ends up with you, Kelsey." He set his glass on the table, his expression turning serious. "Do you think it'd be possible to go back to the very beginning? To that day in the church when we first met?"

"I was only trying to find a way out of the building, but I found you instead." She stuck out her hand. "Name's Kelsey. Nice to meet you."

Instead of taking her hand, Park leaned forward and kissed her on the mouth, long and hard. "The pleasure's all mine," he said at last.

CHAPTER 17

The next morning dawned hot and bright and glorious. Kelsey rose early and tiptoed down the hall, past Park's sleeping form on the living room couch.

He'd insisted on staying over for the night. Said she needed a bodyguard to make sure nothing else happened to her. Then he grabbed two of the largest pillows from the sofa's back and tossed them on the ground, proclaiming the couch to be his bed for the night. He was such a southern gentleman. *Damn.*

She passed behind the couch, quietly, so as not to wake him. The kitchen abutted the living room, so there was no way she could turn on the coffee maker without rousing him. He deserved to rest—they both did—but somehow she felt more energized than she had in days. Simply knowing who killed Becca Cooper had released tension from her shoulders, which she hadn't been aware of until it was gone. It felt good to greet the morning again. Good to see the line of cherries dancing along the kitchen backsplash, to watch the sun warm the walls to a buttery gold, to hear the cicadas outside practicing their scales for the day. As cheesy as it might have sounded, it felt good to be alive after what could have happened the day before.

She headed back to the bedroom, resisting the urge to lay her hand on Park's cheek as she passed, and quickly threw on a pair of shorts and her favorite t-shirt. If she couldn't fix something for them in her kitchen, she could always rely on the Grande Burrito for some good takeout. Thinking about Bernie's huevos rancheros spurred her to grab her car keys and silently slip out the front door.

When she saw that someone had brought her car back to the house for her and parked it at the curb, she paused. There, in the mellow light of morning, the crushed metal, the clawed paint, the shattered blinker all looked even uglier than before. She glanced away before the sight could upset her and slid behind the wheel of the mangled car. Thank goodness it fired up right away, and she headed out for Fifth Street and the Grande Burrito.

This time when she entered the plate-glass door, Bernie immediately rushed to her side, leaving the till of his cash register wide open. Sweeping her into a bear hug, he squeezed her so tightly, she yelped.

"Kelsey!" he bellowed in her ear, ignoring the other patrons in the restaurant.

"You're squishing me." Kelsey tried to wiggle away from his suffocating embrace. Heaven only knew what he would have done if Harris had actually hurt her. "I'm okay, really." She settled into a chair when Bernie finally released her.

"I guess I'm excited to see you in one piece." Still neglecting the gaping cash register, Bernie pulled out the chair next to hers. "Tell me everything. I saw Renee this morning, but she only had some of the details."

"First things first." Kelsey nodded to the register on the display case, and Bernie sheepishly rose and slammed it shut.

"Now, tell me everything," he said when he returned to the table, plunking his elbows down and cupping his chin in his hand like a little boy waiting for storytime.

"What did you hear?" She could only imagine what people were saying now that Harris had been taken away.

"Everyone knows Harris tried to hurt you, but you gave that idiot a whooping." Bernie's eyes shone as he spoke.

"That part's true. He probably had a concussion from the knockout. I used a flower pot on his front porch."

"Good for you, girl. He should have known better than to mess with you."

"What else do you know? Did you know that Harris killed Becca because she was going to have his child?"

Bernie whistled, long and low. "Hadn't heard that part yet. All anyone here knew was that Harris went after Becca, but things got ugly when she told him no."

"Ugly enough for him to kill her and dump her body on the bayou," Kelsey said. "He had no idea Shawn Deschamps would find the body. He probably figured animals would take care of the evidence."

"That's the amazing thing." Bernie shook his head. "Shawn was getting his stuff back together, and he promised his dad and me he wouldn't skip school anymore. But that morning, he said he had a funny feeling he needed to go out there, even though he had no idea why."

"Guess we all know why now." Kelsey glanced down at the empty plate in front of her and at her bone-dry coffee cup. "I came here to get some breakfast to go, but I would kill for some of your coffee right about now."

"Don't use those words around here," he said, only half in jest. "The only thing that needs to be killed are the rumors about Shawn, or even the Holidays, having anything at all to do with the murder."

"Sounds good to me." She pointed to the empty cup. "But I still need a caffeine fix or things are going to get messy around here."

"You got it. Waiter!" Bernie called in the direction of the serape. The blanket wavered and a figure in black emerged.

It was Shawn Deschamps with a shiny silver pot in his hand and a huge grin on his face.

"Yes, sir." He poured some coffee into Kelsey's mug. "Couldn't hear the door open with the water running in the sink."

"Shawn's the best waiter I've ever had." Bernie looked so proud, watching the teenager.

"So you put up with this guy on purpose? That must be some deal he's giving you."

"It is," Shawn agreed. "Me and the band get to play here every weekend. My dad even said he'd pay for music school if I stick with this gig."

What do you know? "That's wonderful! Hey, Shawn. Can I get two orders of huevos rancheros to go?"

"Yes, ma'am." The boy left them, but before returning to the back, he stopped at a nearby table to refill the other patrons' coffee cups. It could have been her imagination, but he seemed to be walking a little taller now, his head held high.

"Two orders? Why, Kelsey. I didn't think you were that kind of girl."

"Save it, Bernie. Park came home with me to make sure I was okay. He's on my couch right now, so I don't want to hear any lectures."

Bernie rose and backed away. "None of my business. None of my business at all. By the way, he likes his eggs scrambled, not fried."

She watched Bernie disappear behind the serape, and finally took a long drink from the coffee mug. Much as she wanted to rush right back to the cottage and the sleeping form on her sofa, something about being so near to the newsroom next door tugged at her. She had unfinished business there. She could feel it in her soul: a hollowness that wouldn't let her relax quite yet. She set the mug down on the table. "Hold that order for a little bit, okay?" she yelled to the men behind the serape. "Give me ten minutes or so, and I'll come back for it."

Bernie didn't respond, but she was confident he'd heard her, so she left the restaurant and emerged onto Fifth Street. By now it was nine o'clock, so she knew the newsroom would be open and she'd find Renee behind her desk, working away.

Sure enough, the overheads already had been flicked on when she swept through the front door. Renee sat in front of her monitor, like always, squinting at something or other on the screen.

"Kelsey!" She finally looked up when the sleigh bells stopped jangling. "Didn't expect to see you here so soon. What's up? Tell me everything." Renee pushed her chair away from the desk and turned her back on the computer screen.

"Can't right now. But I'll be back," she promised as she headed for her own desk and the filing cabinet next to it.

"Not so fast. Some guy keeps trying to call you. Must have tried three times just this morning. He didn't want to talk to me. The number's on your desk."

Kelsey glanced at the desktop, where Renee had placed three ice-blue telephone messages. Picking up the first one, she saw "Jason Lee" scrawled across the top of it. Sure enough, the second and third notes had the very same information written in the same impatient scrawl.

"Whoever it is, he sounded determined. Wanted you to call him as soon as you came in."

Kelsey sank into the chair at her desk, realizing the importance of this moment bit by bit. This wasn't a random telephone call she could ignore until she returned to work. This was Jason Lee, the editor at the biggest newspaper in Dallas, and the one person on the planet she never expected to call amid the chaos around her. In fact, she had half-hoped the telephone calls had been made by Park, though he was probably still sleeping on her living room sofa.

"I'll call him." She reached for the telephone, but paused

when she realized Renee had yet to return to her work. She had no idea what she was going to say to Mr. Lee. As awkward as the moment felt, the last thing she needed was an audience. "Do you mind?"

Renee shrugged and swiveled around in her chair. "Sorry. Forget I'm even here. I'll be quiet as a ghost, I swear."

Kelsey made a second pass at the telephone. She had memorized the editor's telephone number after staring at the note for the past minute, so she punched in the numbers without consulting the scrap of blue paper. After two rings, a familiar, albeit clipped, voice came on the line.

"Jason Lee."

Unlike her first call to the Dallas newsroom, the editor had given her his private number so she didn't have to go through an assistant or a reporter to reach him. Which meant he was serious about whatever he had to say.

"Hi, Mr. Lee. I'm returning your call. It's Kelsey Garrett."

"Miss Garrett." He sounded jovial now, as if he had been expecting her call and was relieved it had finally arrived. "You're not easy to get ahold of."

She cleared her throat, buying time if nothing else. "There's no way you could know this, but I was out yesterday because of the murder investigation here." All of which would make no difference to someone sitting hundreds of miles away, but to Kelsey it was an incredible statement to make.

"I understand. Do they have the guy now? Your story said something about the local pastor in town, and that's who I'm putting my money on."

"Well, you would lose, then." She didn't want to sound flippant, but it was a tad annoying that a total stranger had already crowned Reverend Holiday the murderer, though she realized that her news stories hadn't done anything to dispel that notion. All that would change, though, when she wrote a follow-up

217

for the next issue of the paper. "It was someone else at the church. A deacon. He's in custody right now. Turns out he got a nasty concussion in a scuffle."

"Well, what do you know? Hey . . . I read that story you sent over. Not bad. Not bad at all."

Everything seemed to slow at that point as the line fell silent. Did the editor just tell her he liked her writing? Maybe she'd misunderstood. "Excuse me?"

"I want you to come up to Dallas for a real interview. We'll take care of the airline and hotel if you can get yourself up here in the next day or two."

Now she knew she'd heard correctly. Her heartbeat did jumping jacks as she processed the news. "You're kidding, right? You want me to come there. Tomorrow?" These newsmen moved so fast they made her head spin. She looked helplessly from the telephone to Renee, who had given up all pretense of minding her own business and now watched her every move.

"Yes, if you can manage it. I have an opening in the newsroom I need to fill right away. We could do the interview in the morning, it that's okay with you."

"It's not that." Her voice faltered. By now Renee looked ready to burst with curiosity, bent forward in her chair like that. It wasn't that at all. He could have offered Kelsey an interview next week, or next month, or next year, and still, she would have faltered. It was all too much. There was a perfectly wonderful man waiting for her not five miles away. A restaurant owner next door who had squeezed the life out of her when he found out she was safe. Renee, who had become so much more than an editor to her over the past six months. Now a stranger was asking her to put all this behind her. This is what she had wanted, right? Swimming pools, movie stars. A chance to say good-bye to small-town Texas and move to the big city. What was she waiting for?

"I can't." The minute she spoke, the pounding in her chest stilled. "Thank you, but I can't."

"You realize this is the first opening I've had in months," he told her crisply. "Newspapers are laying people off, not giving them jobs. You might want to reconsider."

As she listened to the editor, she glanced across the newsroom and saw the scraggly hound dog from the week before, lumbering along the sidewalk, right in front of the newsroom's window. Probably still searching for that overturned dumpster. No one said that Enterprise was perfect, but odds were good the starving dog would find some leftovers waiting for him in the alley behind Bernie's restaurant. No, this town wasn't perfect. But it was home. "I've made up my mind. Thank you for the offer, but I'm not interested. Good-bye." With that, she replaced the telephone on the receiver.

"What was that all about?" If Renee had an inkling something was afoot, she managed a wonderful poker face.

"Somebody wanting me to do something. I said I'd pass.' Kelsey left it at that. After all, what was one secret between friends?

"Get back to work, you slacker," Renee teased. "You've got a feature to write, and unless you've trained your computer to copywrite for you, it's time to get busy."

That sounded good. Very good. She knew exactly what she'd include in her final story about the case. It did feel as if the piece might write itself.

Still . . . there was someone waiting for her back home and a hot breakfast coming due next door. Everything could wait now. Now she had all the time in the world.

ABOUT THE AUTHOR

Sandra Bretting is a freelance feature writer for the *Houston Chronicle*, and also writes for several companies around town. Her short stories have appeared in *BorderSenses Literary Magazine*, produced by the University of Texas at El Paso, the 2009 anthology *My Mom Is My Hero*, and other publications. Nonfiction credits include the *Los Angeles Times* and *Woman's Day*. Visit www.sandrabretting.com for information about new releases and upcoming book events.